Tara Pammi can't remember a moment when she wasn't lost in a book—especially a romance, which was much more exciting than a mathematics textbook at school. Years later, Tara's wild imagination and love for the written word revealed what she really wanted to do. Now she pairs alpha males who think they know everything with strong women who knock that theory *and* them off their feet!

Discover more at millsandboon.co.uk

BOUGHT
WITH THE
ITALIAN'S RING

BY
TARA PAMMI

MILLS & BOON

First Published in Great Britain 2018
by Mills & Boon, an imprint of HarperCollins*Publishers*
1 London Bridge Street, London, SE1 9GF

© 2018 Tara Pammi

ISBN: 978-0-263-93408-3

MIX
Paper from
responsible sources
FSC **FSC® C007454**
www.fsc.org

This book is produced from independently certified FSC™ paper
to ensure responsible forest management.
For more information visit www.harpercollins.co.uk/green.

Printed and bound in Spain
by CPI, Barcelona

CHAPTER ONE

HER SKIN PRICKLED. Her body, even though overheated from two hours of dancing, suddenly tingled.

Pia Vito could almost pinpoint the moment the piercing awareness claimed her, the moment a sudden chill replaced the warm breeze coming in through the wide doors of the vast ballroom on her grandfather's estate.

It was the moment *he* walked in.

Raphael Mastrantino.

Her grandfather Giovanni's godson and protégé.

CEO of Vito Automobiles.

The man Milanese society seems to be in awe of.

The women around her went into a quiet frenzy, sending longing looks his way, detailing his finer points to each other.

From the moment she had discovered her long-lost grandfather Gio, and he had accepted her as his granddaughter at the beginning of the summer, all Pia had heard from him was stories about Raphael Mastrantino.

And her drama-prone grandfather hadn't exaggerated for once.

No other man could have prowled inside the ballroom with such arrogant confidence, as if he owned the estate and all the people in it.

No other man would look that striking in a plain white shirt while making the rest of the tuxedo-clad men look overdressed.

No other man could have commanded the attention of an entire ballroom by his mere presence.

Piercing eyes met hers across the ballroom, held hers, as if determined to see through to her soul.

It was as if an electric arc had built up between them—the very concept she'd been explaining to her fifth grade students back home.

No adjective she knew could describe the sheer masculinity of him. Broad shoulders tapered to a lean waist, long legs. The ruthless planes of his face, the stark angles were those one only saw in sculptures.

It took every ounce of energy she possessed to keep her smile in place.

Not even a facsimile of a greeting appeared in his hard face. With his cynical and appraising expression, even from a distance Pia felt his derision to the tips of her toes.

Any warmth she'd felt amidst the dancing crowd dissipated as realization struck.

Her grandfather's godson didn't *approve* of her? Why?

Which was why she had felt his gaze on her back like a concentrated laser beam.

Ignoring his presence—which was like the earth trying to ignore the sun—her movements awkward and stilted, she adjusted her path exiting the dance floor and kept moving, head down.

She ran straight into something so solidly male her breath jumped into her throat. Cursing herself, she looked up. And was caught in the darkest eyes she had ever seen, draped by the lushest lashes no mascara could ever reproduce.

When had he moved so close?

His fingers had landed on the patch of bare skin that her dress and gloves left on her arms. The pads of his fingers pressed into her flesh, not quite hard but not gently either. As if he knew of her intention to escape him.

The scent of him, warmed by his skin, drifted up toward her nostrils and she breathed in deeply. A furious flush began to work its way from her chest to her neck and upward at his continued scrutiny.

She had never been comfortable with men, had no idea of that subtle, sophisticated flirting language all her fellow teachers, at least the young ones, seemed to know. Even with Frank, it had taken her two months to put a sentence together.

But this felt as if she were naked, as if her worst fears—her loneliness after her grandmother's death, her overwhelming need to belong somewhere, anywhere—as if it were all on display for his eyes.

"You are not running away from me, are you, *cara mia*?" came a taunt in the deep, silky voice that let loose butterflies in her stomach.

When she'd banged into him, she had braced herself with her hands and there they rested now. On him. His abdomen, to be precise. He was a granite wall under her hands. She fluttered her fingers over him, curious to see if there would be softness, if she could find more give…

The pressure of his fingers increased over her wrists, arresting her explorations. "Do you not speak then?" This time, he sounded coldly angry. "You communicate instead by touching men?"

Pia pulled back as if burned.

This was ridiculous. She managed twenty eleven-year-olds every day in the classroom! How dare he give voice to something so embarrassing, something she'd only done as a reaction to stress?

"My head hurts," she somehow managed to say and it was partly true. "I'm not used to so much jewelry. The designer heels I'm wearing are killing my feet. Please excuse me."

"How charmingly you lie, Ms. Vito."

He delivered the insult in such a smooth voice that it took her a few seconds to realize it.

"Next, you will tell me you hate these kinds of parties and you were just putting on a good show for Gio's sake. That the jewelry and dress and shoes—the ones that incidentally proclaim you as a walking fortune—are not really *your thing*." He twisted the last two words into a mocking American twang. "That you didn't really enjoy dancing with every man who asked you with that innocent invitation in your eyes. That this whole evening is an elaborate charade you're suffering through like a good sacrificial lamb."

That was exactly what she had been doing.

The dress, the shoes, the jewelry, even the complicated updo her hair was twisted into, none of it was her. But she had kept quiet.

Because she'd wanted Giovanni to be proud of her.

Because she'd wanted to be someone else, even for one night. Sophisticated and charming and polished—not a woman who fell for lies and found herself in crushing debt.

Yet this arrogant man made it sound as if the idea of Pia not wanting the attention, not liking being on display were impossible.

"You've already drawn your conclusions, Mr. Mastrantino."

"How do you know who I am?"

"Gio told me you'd be the most handsome, the most powerful and the most arrogant man I've ever met. He was right." Heat climbed up her chest as he raised a brow.

She looked around the ballroom and every pair of eyes was trained on them. Locating her grandfather's silver hair, she sent him a *please-rescue-me* look.

As if he hadn't even seen her, Gio carried on his conversation.

A pulse of panic drummed through her. It was as if Mr.

Mastrantino, Gio and even the guests were playing a game, but no one had told Pia the rules.

"Then you have the advantage, for he told me nothing about you. Until I saw the invitation, I didn't even know you existed. A ball in honor of Pia Alessandra Vito." He was a few inches taller than even her uncommon height and for the first time in her life, Pia felt dainty, even fragile. "Giovanni's long-lost granddaughter, finally returned to the bosom of her loving family, his legacy displayed like a crowning jewel to society."

Why was he so *ticked off* with her?

But his possessive touch stilled everything within her. Her breath hitched, and her insides seemed intent upon some kind of rearrangement. Like molecules under heat.

"The Cinderella story of the year," he continued, a hardness in the curve of his sensual mouth. "I assume Gio has already also *bought* a prince for you to dance with before the stroke of midnight too, *si*?"

Bought a prince for her?

As if a man had to be paid to be with her! Pia could feel the color leaching from her face.

Raphael had no idea how deep his thoughtless comment dug into her. How much it hurt.

"Gio knows I don't want a…" The words stilled as she tallied all the men that had been hounding her tonight.

Why had Gio invited so many young, eligible men? Why had each and every one of them made a beeline for her? True, she was the guest of honor, but still. There were other women at the ball.

A shiver curled around her spine.

"Non?" Raphael inflected it enough to tell her he didn't believe her. "Why do you think all these men have been falling over themselves to dance with you? Your great beauty?" His gaze raked her, and then dismissed her. "Your charming conversation? Your magnetic presence?"

With each derogatory question out of his mouth, Pia knew he had it right. But she was damned if she would stand there another moment and let him mock her.

She turned and stumbled. A pained gasp fell from her mouth.

Strong arms wound around her waist from behind before her bottom kissed the black-and-white marble floor. His muscular forearms brushed the undersides of her breasts, pushing them up. A burst of heat filled her lower belly.

Pia clung to him, her breath in disarray. It was too much sensation, too raw.

Slowly, gently, as if she were a newborn calf, he turned her around. In a movement that was as fluid as it was economic, he knelt in front of her.

Her heart pounded.

A pin could have dropped in the ballroom and it would have been an explosion.

His trousers stretched tight over his thighs, his austere face raised to her, he cradled her foot in a tender clasp. A lock of his thick black hair fell forward on his forehead. Those dark eyes moved over her face, down her throat, where her pulse pounded violently, to the sight of the upper curves of her meager breasts plumped into fullness by the bodice.

A tightness emerged in his face.

Tilting his head down, he placed her right foot on his left thigh. The tips of her fingers rested on his shoulders and she felt the muscles there shift and clench.

With uncharacteristic malice, she hoped the pointed heel would bruise his rock-hard flesh.

His fingers unbuckled the small belt of her sandal with a nimble touch. He plucked the heel off her foot, and fingers wrapped around her bare flesh.

Pia flinched as pain and awareness mingled, spreading up from her ankle.

His nostrils flared, his mouth pinching into a stiff line. Long fingers rubbed the small ridge the strap had dug into her skin. Back and forth, softly, slowly, until a soft moan— a raw, unrestrained sound—fell from her mouth.

Holding her gaze, he touched her more boldly, more purposefully.

A strange, forbidden craving released in her lower belly, warmth pooling there. Her heart beat in rhythm to those fingers. When he moved one finger upward, almost reaching her knee, Pia jerked her foot back.

And then, because of the uneven balance, toppled onto him.

With a curse, he caught her. But he was still so tall that when she fell, his face was buried scandalously against her belly. The warmth of his breath against her soft muscles set off such a deep clench in her sex that Pia whimpered.

His hands on her waist, he gave her a gentle nudge. Her entire body was a shivering, needy pulse. Pia looked down at his hands. "Let me go."

He shrugged those broad shoulders, an innocent look in his eyes. "You will fall if I let you go."

This man was dangerous. What he so easily made her feel—this hitch of her breath, this nervous knot in her belly, the warmth unspooling in every muscle—every forbidden sensation was dangerous.

This time, instead of putting her foot on his thigh, she put her hand on his shoulder, balanced herself and shed her other sandal. Then she picked them up with her left hand, muttered a rushed *thanks* at his shoulder and straightened.

She moved no more than a couple of steps when he stood in front of her again. "It is not the stroke of midnight yet, so surely it is not time for you to disappear, is it?"

Pia faced him, still shuddering after that intimate slide against him. Hard and lean and unforgiving, his body had left an imprint on hers. "You're no prince. More like the devil."

A white smile flashed in his dark face.

Pia sighed. The man's will was unbending. Her feet hurt, her head was throbbing, she really was tired. But of course, her grandfather's godson had come to the ball with an agenda.

He turned her around with his hands on her shoulders and gently pushed her to the center of the dance floor. One arrogant nod of his head and the orchestra began playing a classical waltz.

One large hand spanned her waist while the other clasped her fingers. Her body stretched tight and stiff to resist gliding against his. For a few minutes, they moved around the floor seamlessly, yet she couldn't relax, couldn't muster a single calm breath. His scent weaved around her. He was hard and lean everywhere she touched him.

"My ego would suffer if I didn't already know that you are just as stiff and awkward with other men," he whispered against her ear while his arm rested around her waist.

Pia found herself sinking into the depths of those black eyes. She was plain and awkward, yes, but no coward. "I'm sure I could hardly dent that humongous ego."

His laughter, a deep, husky sound startled the life out of her.

Of course, graceful dancer that he was, he didn't let his own steps falter.

Long fingers fluttered near the underside of her breast making Pia aware of every inch of her skin. "Tell me about yourself." For all her supposed resistance, he had somehow pulled her closer. On a side step, her hip rubbed against his thigh. Pia shivered. "About your dreams and aspirations," he continued, as if he felt nothing of the torture he put her through. As if he felt nothing *period*. "Maybe your favorite ice cream or your favorite Italian designer. Or what you're planning to ask Gio to give you for your birthday present."

"Birthday present?"

"You know, to make up for all the years he missed. A yacht? Are you fond of sailing? A condo in Venice?"

"I've no idea—"

Another turn around the hall, but this time with the sensation of his palm covering her upper back. She couldn't take much more of this heightened awareness. "How old are you?"

"Twenty-three."

"Quite an accomplishment for one so young."

Her body was so aware of him that her mind couldn't grapple with the intent in his words. "Please, stop. Just stop. I'm not…good at this."

His thumb traced the veins over the back of her hand almost absently. "What is the *this* that you're not good at?"

"Dealing with men like you. Playing ridiculous games. I'm not like other women you probably know. I'm nothing like the women I know."

His gaze swept over the tiara in her hair, the diamonds at her throat. "I would say you're doing just fine. From everything I see, you have Giovanni wrapped around your finger."

"I don't know how to decipher your words. I don't understand why you're determined to make a spectacle of me in this crowd. I don't know why you're—"

Her attraction to Gio's godson was the last thing she needed. Especially when, clearly, he bore no goodwill toward her.

A finger under her chin, he tilted her face up to look at him. The stark beauty of him hit her hard again. "Why I'm what?"

"Why you're even touching me like this… I don't know

why I'm reacting to you like this. Why my heart is beating so hard I feel like it might rip out of my chest. Why there's this…" His eyes flared and Pia caught the words that were bent on pouring out of her mouth. "And why you're so intent on proving that you affect me like that even as your eyes are full of contempt."

His mouth lost that cynical curve; his eyes became searching, intent. It seemed she had finally shocked him.

His hold gentled and Pia slipped away. The marble floor was cold against her bare feet reminding her she had left her heels behind.

But she was no more Cinderella than Raphael Mastrantino was a prince.

Raphael ran a finger along his collar, his body humming with awareness, with unspent energy as if he were a randy youth.

His attraction to Pia—instant and all consuming—defied logic. She was not beautiful, not in the conventional sense, not sophisticated for all her dress and jewelry—and yet there was something irresistibly alluring about her.

Which woman among the society he lived in would so openly admit what she felt for him? And with that artless dismay that she was attracted to him?

No, first there were games, games that every woman played. Even his mother played them when Raphael refused to buy her the latest model of the Vito Viva. Either she cooked his favorite food every night or she shed phony tears over his father's death—an entire episode meant to guilt him and remind him that he should be a good son who granted each and every one of her expensive wishes.

Even his four sisters played games, with Raphael, and with their boyfriends who had inevitably turned into husbands.

No one admitted in that raw, unsophisticated way what

a man made her feel. No one moaned like that—as if she were sinking into a whirlpool of pleasure when a man touched her ankle. No woman that he knew stared at a man with those big, luminous eyes as if he was the answer to her every fantasy.

Coy looks, innuendoes laced with sexual tension, teases, throwing herself at other men to make him jealous—the list of things his ex-wife, Allegra, had tried on him a few years ago were innumerable.

I'm not good at playing games.

There had been a genuine quality to her distress, to her confusion. As if her body was betraying her and she didn't know what to do.

Either she was truly naive—an anachronism with her faint blushes and her trembling mouth—or she knew just how to appeal to a man as jaded and cynical as he was. Perhaps she had decided that the right way to court his attention would be to cater to that traditional man in him, the Neanderthal that Allegra had called him so many times.

Was that it? Had she thought to counter his distrust by catering precisely to his tastes?

A chill ran down the length of his spine as he made his usual rounds through the mansion as he usually did when visiting.

He had no doubt about how much Gio would have talked about him over the last month. As his godson and his protégé, he was Giovanni's pride and joy. Raphael had turned the small spare automobile parts company that Gio had handed him into Vito Automobiles, a leading manufacturing company.

Giovanni had been his lifeline when he'd been sinking as a seventeen-year-old. He'd been a light in a long, dark tunnel that Raphael's weak father had plunged them all into.

Not that it stopped Giovanni from also being manipulative as hell. Throughout the evening, he had stood on the periphery of the crowd, watching, with a satisfied smile on his face. Like a puppeteer intensely delighted with the results of his string pulling.

Whatever the old man was up to, it would eventually fall to Raphael to clean it up. Just as he kept Giovanni's hounding relatives at bay. Just as he ensured that the leftovers from Gio's time on the board—men who would stab Raphael in the back before he could blink—didn't leach away the gains he had made.

Just as he took care of the various and sundry branches of Mastrantino families without any expectations in return.

And yet, as he questioned one of the staff members about Pia, Raphael was suddenly aware that this was unlike any other responsibility he shouldered.

For no bickering ex-wife of Gio's or grasping cousin of his mother had ever caused his blood to pound like this.

No woman had ever called to his baser instincts like this supposedly innocent granddaughter of his godfather.

CHAPTER TWO

COOL WATER SLUICED off her back and limbs as Pia swam lap after lap in the indoor pool on Gio's estate as if the very devil were after her.

Raphael Mastrantino was very much the devil.

The man's arrogance!

She worked off her fury in the water.

Of all the men to be attracted to.

She groaned and dunked her head in the water. He'd been so warm and solid around her. She could still feel the languorous weight of his hands on her waist. The length of his hard thigh rubbing against hers...

The only satisfaction left to her was that she'd surprised him even as he had mocked and taunted her.

She and Raphael Mastrantino lived in different orbits of life. He wouldn't have even looked at her, much less danced with her, if she hadn't been dressed up to the nines *and* if she wasn't Gio's granddaughter. What she didn't understand though was why. Why had he pounced on her like that?

Her arms lagged on her strokes as her thoughts whirled. Just as she decided to get out of the pool, she saw Raphael standing at the edge.

The floodlights cast an outline along his broad frame.

His white shirt was unbuttoned to the middle of his chest giving a glimpse of ridges of tight muscle with sparse black hair. Her belly swooped. The raven's wing of his hair had a distinctly rumpled look.

What would it take to shatter that arrogant cynicism, to bring a man like Raphael to his knees?

She shivered at the direction of her thoughts.

A bottle of Pinot Grigio and two wine flutes hung from his fingers. "I had to bribe one of the staff members for your location."

"I don't like you, Mr. Mastrantino."

"I think you like me a little too much. Which is why you're hiding."

The gall of the man! Pia had never met a more annoying man in her life. "Just because my body thinks you're a prime male specimen and is attracted to you—which, by the way, is based on millions of years of evolution and a chemical reaction that drives a woman to choose the strongest man as her mate—it doesn't mean my mind agrees."

His black eyes gleamed. The thin line of his lower lip curved with mocking amusement. "So you've dropped the act of trembling mouth and soft gasps then?"

He almost sounded disappointed. Pia sighed. "Distance helped me remember the hormones part of it. It's when you're close that I…" She shrugged, trying to go for casual, which her stutter totally ruined. "That I'm unable to handle my reaction."

Just looking at the darkly sensual face stretched her skin tight over her body. And other parts. Parts that had never clenched and tightened with such wanton awareness.

"You should call me Raphael."

"Not necessary."

He placed the bottle and glasses on a table then settled on a lounger, propped his elbows on his knees and returned to his intense scrutiny of her. "Because you'll run away every time I'm around?"

"I've been suitably and repeatedly impressed with what an important, powerful and wealthy man you are. You run a multinational automobile company in the city, apparently control and manage not only Gio's finances but your mother's family' finances and your father's and all the numerous cousins thereof.

I, on the other hand, mean to spend the summer getting to know Gio. I let him railroad me into this ball because it meant a lot to him. So the chance of you and me spending time in each other's company is pretty low."

"When the summer is over?" he shot back instantly, picking the one thing Pia didn't want to discuss.

"This summer is just holiday. I wasn't even sure if Gio would believe me. But I do have a life elsewhere." A life without her grandmother, a life without any close friends. A life where no one really cared about her.

Which was why she'd been such an easy mark for Frank.

"Is Gio aware of your supposed intentions?"

"No, and they're not supposed," she said, losing her temper. Would nothing please the man?

The water lapped around her silently. "You're staring," she said softly.

"You look like a different woman."

"I was terrified all evening that I'd spill something on that gorgeous, expensive gown. I have a habit of getting into worse messes than my students. I'm not used to wearing contacts. Now there is no war paint on my face. And my hair is back in its natural, uncontrollable state." She pulled a coiled curl that was already dry.

He followed the action as if he was transfixed. "Your students?"

"I teach Science to fifth graders."

Surprise dawned in his gaze. It tracked her wet face, lingering far too long than was proper over her mouth, and then the slope of her shoulders, visible over the water's surface. A shiver snaked down her spine.

"An elementary teacher? I find I'm overwhelmed by curiosity about you. A rare occurrence."

Pia stared, wishing she'd misheard him. But the world was quiet around them. Only a slight breeze and the whispers of the trees all around the pool. It wasn't just curiosity that made his voice deepen, that made his mouth tighten.

"What do you have against me?"

Moonlight caressed the dark column of his throat, the smooth velvety skin pulled taut over a lean chest. He tilted his head down, a devilish twist to his mouth. "Other than the fact that you're manipulating an old man's misguided affection for you?"

His words shocked Pia so much that she dropped her hold on the tiles, sank in, and then came up sputtering water out of her nose and mouth.

He thought she was after Gio's fortune?

He frowned at her chattering teeth. "Get out of there before you freeze."

"No," Pia said stubbornly, a rush of anger heating up her still muscles. "*You* leave."

His hands went to the buttons on his shirt. Taut skin stretched over lean muscles appeared as he unbuttoned. "Either you come out or…"

Glaring at him, Pia walked up the steps.

The moment she was out, he wrapped the huge towel around her. Heart thundering in her chest, Pia pushed her wet hair off her face with trembling hands.

As if she were a child, he gave her a brisk rubdown, up and down her arms. Throat dry, Pia stared at his chest. Her cheeks burned when he repeated the movements over her chest, hips and back. Those large hands didn't linger anywhere and yet warmth began to pool in her belly.

"You stayed too long in there." His voice had gone husky, deep.

She shivered again.

"Sit," he commanded, and Pia obediently sat on the lounger. He handed her a glass of wine and it was exactly what she wanted.

Silently, she took a sip.

For a few minutes, they sat like that, side by side on loungers, not talking. Not even looking at each other. But that awareness that had consumed her in the ballroom thickened the air around them. His touch, impersonal, still lingered.

Her attraction to him was natural.

He *was* the most strikingly handsome man she'd ever met.

She refused to be ashamed by it. But neither did she want to keep confronting it, to keep thinking that she was somehow less than him because she wasn't sophisticated or beautiful or polished enough. She'd had enough of Frank manipulating her insecurities. "All I want is to spend the summer with my grandfather. I really don't see why that should be any of your business," she said softly.

"I am Giovanni's friend. I am more friend than all of his useless, bickering, social climbing family put together. I would do anything to protect Giovanni and his interests. It is my business if you put one step wrong with him."

"What have I done that offends you so much?"

"You seem to have no scruples about cheating an old man who has done nothing but welcome you into his life with open arms without even checking if you truly are who you claim to be."

"So now I'm not only a gold digger of the worst kind but also an impostor?"

"All evidence points to it, *si*."

Pia fisted her hands, the urge to strike that smug condescension from his face burning through her. "Gio's lover, Lucia, was my *nonna*. She left him after they had a huge row and settled in the States. My parents died when I was three and she raised me." She stood up, her pulse skittering all over. "I found Lucia's letters to him after she died and called him. That's the truth."

"It's also true that he's given you thousands of dollars in the one month you've been here."

If only the ground could open up and swallow her whole! Mortification filled her cheeks.

She couldn't even be mad at Raphael, because from his point of view it looked like she was a grasping, greedy woman. But to be so cynical as to question her whole motive for visiting Italy…? "Gio wouldn't have told you," she mumbled half to herself.

"I keep an eye over Gio's finances. His three ex-wives learned it was better to live with what he provides them than to take me on."

She forced herself to meet his eyes. "You're making assumptions based on one transaction and out of context."

"I assume based on facts and not feelings. I learned to do so a long time ago."

The towel slipped from her shoulders so her hair was dripping onto her back. And the one-piece she wore was not the most convenient costume when wet. But Pia was determined to make him see. Even if it meant admitting the most humiliatingly painful episode of her life. Even if it meant giving voice to her foolishness. "Giovanni gave me that money to pay off…credit card debt."

"So you did your research before you contacted him," he said in a silky, almost bored voice.

Her grip far too tight on the stem of the wineglass Pia stared at him. "This is pointless if you won't even give me a chance.

"You have to protect Giovanni, true, but one would think you'd at least give me a chance when his happiness is involved." She wouldn't beg him to believe her. Shaking with hurt and humiliation, she stood up.

He reached out and caught her wrist. A jolt of fiery sensation raced from her wrist to her breasts, to the spot between her thighs. Pia jerked her hand away, breath coming in hard and fast.

"Stay." Tension radiated from him, confusing her. "I will listen, *si*? Whether I will believe…"

She sat down and looked at her hands. Words came and fell away again. Taking a deep breath, she blurted it out. "I racked up that debt because I was foolish enough to fall for a con man."

His expression instantly turned thunderous. "Fall for a con man? What do you mean?"

"I believed a colleague when he said he loved me. I went back to work after nursing Nonni for two years and he was the new gym teacher at the school where I worked. He… cultivated a friendship with me for weeks, then asked me out. After a few months, he…told me he'd fallen in love with me.

'I trusted him and loaned him money when he said he was in trouble. Again and again. I gave him the little Nonni had left me, and then when that was done, I…" The words stuck like glass in her throat. "I emptied my savings, and took a loan on my card when he said he desperately needed money to avoid a loan shark."

His expletive punctured the silence around them. Did that mean he believed her? Pia found she didn't give a damn. Frank had deceived her in the worst possible way. Nothing Raphael said or believed could be any worse.

There was a strange strength in the fact that she'd already been through the worst.

"So you're as naive and meek as you look? How could you trust any man so much that you risk everything you have?"

She flinched as if he'd slapped her. Tight lines emerged around her mouth and she blinked rapidly. Moonlight flickered on her delicate jawline that was clenched taut.

Raphael killed the thread of regret that hit him. He wasn't going to coddle her.

She looked down at her hands and then around her. When she spoke, her voice had lost that husky timbre. It was as if she was forcing herself to say the words. Just for his benefit.

"I was lost, lonely after Nonni passed away. I hardly had any friends after being her full-time caregiver for two years. He was charming, attractive. He singled me out almost immediately after I went back to work. He even did me the favor of explaining to me that he had done his research and picked me as the prime target. The other teachers had unwittingly given him enough ammunition."

Even as he'd cruelly called her weak, she was anything but in that moment. He knew that it took guts to pull yourself up when everything was lost. And yet, she'd not only done it, but she was facing him down too. "How?"

"They told him that I was…shy, and inexperienced. That they thought I needed to start living now that Nonni had passed away. They told him I'd never had a boyfriend and would probably be grateful for his attention." When he growled, she hurried on. "I think they meant well. They couldn't have known he would prey on all my insecurities."

"This man? Is he following you here?"

"No." Conviction resonated in her tone. "When he realized I didn't have any more money, he couldn't dump me fast enough. Making it very clear that the only reason he'd been with me was because I was such a pushover."

"So you didn't tell him about how your new grandfather was wealthy beyond imagination? No surprise visit from this lover of yours to play upon Gio's heartstrings a little more? Have you already figured out that Gio's an old fool who would love to see a little romance?"

"Stop, please. He's not coming here. Frank's out of my life," Pia replied, a sick feeling in her stomach. She could see what Raphael was getting at. And that his suspicions had basis only increased her shame. "For one thing, I didn't know until I got here that Gio was wealthy. I don't care whether you believe that or not," she pushed on, when she sensed he would interrupt again. *Blasted man!* "I was just happy to know that I had family. That I wasn't alone…"

How could she make him understand how lonely she had been after Nonni's death? How much Frank had played on that loneliness?

Or what Gio's affection, his kindness meant to her. "And, yes, I'll even admit that if Frank had learned that Giovanni Vito *is* Vito Automobiles, he probably would've—" she forced herself to say the horrible words "—married me and sealed off the deal so that he could suck the blood and marrow out of Gio."

She shivered violently. Raphael silently draped another plush towel around her shoulders.

Pia thanked him, the words tasting like ash in her mouth. She didn't want his kindness. She didn't want anything from this man.

"I need details about this Frank person."

She nodded. "Will you leave me alone then?"

"What Giovanni did—"

"The money he gave me, it's a loan. I didn't take a dollar more than the debt. And I intend to pay off every single cent." She pulled her towel snug around her chest. "Your relationship with Gio, his affection for you, that's the only reason I told you. You and I have nothing to do with each other, Mr. Mastrantino."

* * *

She was wrong.

Whether she was Gio's granddaughter or not, whether she was disconcertingly naive or a cunning con woman, Pia was going to be his problem.

Lashes spiked with small water drops, her damp hair curling wispily against her face, she looked incredibly young. And even with her declaration that she'd learned her lesson, there was still something very naive about her.

It was disconcerting how much he wanted to believe her.

There was grief in those big luminous eyes of hers, an earnestness that beguiled him.

But more than that, he wanted to taste that trembling mouth. He wanted to wrap her tiny waist with his hands and bring her closer until he was wet along with her; until her soft curves brushed up against him.

Until he could kiss away the trouble caused by another man.

He wanted to wrap her in some sort of protective co-coon so that nothing deceitful could touch her.

Dio mio, he had met her five hours ago and even he was already lured in by that innocence. Giovanni would do anything for this creature.

But the fact that she could be telling the truth only made the problem worse.

Not only had Gio had her decked up in diamonds and couture, he had released her into a hungry horde of Milanese social climbers.

At least if she'd been a con woman, she would have been able to handle herself.

He reached for her when she walked by him to leave. Feeling the calluses in her palm, he pulled up her hand.

Her fingers were long and bare, with calluses at the tips of most. He had a sudden flash of Allegra's perfectly manicured nails with baby-soft skin.

"Why do you have calluses?" All this was just to know her, he reminded himself. To create a picture of her life for himself. To see if there were any holes in it. To see if a lie would crack through her elaborate pretense.

Or it's because, for the first time in years, you can't stop yourself from touching a woman. Because the need to touch her, to taste her, is pounding in your blood.

Fingers tracing his palm, sending pulses of heat through him, she frowned. He felt as if he had been earthed. "I could ask you the same. I thought CEOs had pampered, manicured hands and wore tacky, gold bracelets."

A strange, masculine satisfaction whirled through him.

"I'm an automobile engineer first, a CEO second. I restore vintage cars when I find time." He was already stretched superthin as it is and now this—*her.* "Which is very little. Now tell me, why do *you* have calluses?"

"I carve wooden toys in my free time. A hobby really. Frank—" a stiffness thinned her mouth "—set up an on-line shop for me. The cash always came in handy and my students' parents provided good word of mouth."

The man's name on her lips pulled Raphael back to the matter.

She blinked owlishly, as if trying to keep him in focus. He clenched his jaw tight. More pieces were falling into place.

If she was conning all of them, he would see her in jail. But Raphael was forced to rethink his misgivings, to consider Gio's trust might not be misplaced. She knew things about Lucia and Gio that no one did, at least, that was what Gio had told him.

Also, he was a good judge of character.

He'd been forced to be after his father's suicide. He'd had to learn on his feet which creditor could be counted on to wait, which creditor was loyal to his father's tarnished memory and which one would revel in humiliating his mother and sisters if Raphael came up short.

If she was innocent… He could hardly bear thinking about the hordes of hungry, young, single Milanese men that would descend on her… Just tonight, it had taken every ounce of the force of his ruthless reputation to beat off the men who had wanted to follow her.

Men who'd have stood in his place right now and watched moonlight sparkle in her eyes, seen the wet swimsuit cling to her toned, lithe body, seen the artless display of grief and joy that came into her eyes when she spoke of Lucia and Giovanni.

"If I have to carve a million toys to pay Giovanni back, I will," she said with a fierce pride shining in her eyes.

He hardened his tone. "Even if you're telling the truth, I can't just let you walk away without making sure that you've not crushed his heart," he added for good measure.

Her soft sigh pinged over his nerves. Did she know how arousing that was? Did she even realize that the sight of her big, searching gaze, the way she stared at a man as if she meant to see through to his soul, could do things to a man she might not want?

"Why do you think I agreed to that—" she pointed to the house now cloaked in dark shadows "—ridiculous show? Telling Gio about Frank probably wasn't a good idea. All those men he invited, the way they were crowding around me… I didn't realize his intentions until you pointed out how much attention I was getting. Clearly, he thinks I can't take care of myself."

He'd been cruel to taunt her like that. Not that he was off the mark. But there was also an attraction to her that was rare. It was disturbing to think of her coming up against the men who only saw her as a ticket to their life's fortune. "Can you?"

"Even if I can't, the last thing I want is help from a man like you," she bit out, stepping back from him.

He raised a brow. *"A man like me?"*

"My experience with Frank taught me a valuable lesson. My so-called boyfriend that couldn't dump me fast enough when the money dried up. You're just like him—gorgeous, confident, arrogant—except a million times more. The women—they couldn't get enough of you even when you barely glanced in their direction. And the men were so eager to please you, wanting to be like you.

"You...exert your power or charm, or whatever the hell it is, over everyone you meet. You wield it to bend people to your will. Someone like me, you'll use my attraction to you to put me in my place, to prove that you're right no matter what the truth is. To prove that I'm somehow less because I'm not everything you are. Accusations that have no basis in truth, I can handle. But you mock who I am and that I won't forgive."

He felt as if she'd punched him, because it was exactly what he had thought of her. *"Someone like you?"* He repeated her words to hide his reaction.

Pain streaked through her eyes. The depth of her emotions, the sheer transparency of them was like nothing he'd ever seen before.

"A shy, plain, boring elementary teacher who knows nothing about men." She repeated the words as if by rote, and suddenly he knew in his bones who had said them to her. "First you'll use it to dig into me to figure out if I'm telling the truth.

"Then you'll use my lack of sophistication to persuade Gio that he's right and that I need to be wrapped up in bubble wrap because I'm too naive, too foolish. That I'll somehow bring someone like Frank into this...kingdom of yours.

"I don't care whether you believe me or not. Just stay

away from me. We don't have to see each other for you to make sure that I'm not fleecing Gio, do we?"

Her slender shoulders straight, the line of her spine a graceful curve, she looked like a water nymph. Leaving Raphael spellbound in more than one way.

If she was a con woman, he'd see her in jail. But if she was indeed Gio's granddaughter, she was absolutely forbidden to him.

Even if it was the most real conversation he'd had with a woman. Ever.

CHAPTER THREE

STAY AWAY FROM ME.

Pia's words followed him as Raphael walked around the estate and made sure the staff put every last inebriated or otherwise high-flying guest into their vehicles. He bid the tired staff to their beds after they put the ballroom to rights.

He didn't know if Gio thought the ball successful but Raphael thought it had been sensational.

Whoever Pia was, she'd meant those words. His accusations had hurt her, but it was the other thing she'd said that pricked him even now.

You mock who I am.

Had he mocked her because with her naive views and long sighs she'd seemed like an impossibility? Or had he mocked her because he resented that innocence, those stars in her eyes?

Because he'd never had a chance to be like that.

He was about to call it a night and settle into one of the spare bedrooms, as he sometimes did, when he spied the master of puppets.

Scowling, he followed Giovanni into his study and closed the door behind him with a loud thud.

Giovanni handed Raphael a glass of red. As if he'd known that his godson wouldn't leave without this talk.

"Shouldn't you be in bed?" Raphael said as Giovanni plopped down onto the sofa with a long sigh. Because of his agile mind and his penchant for playing games, Raphael sometimes forgot that Gio was old. His wrinkled hands shook as he lifted the glass to his mouth.

"You're far too excited, Giovanni. This is not good—"

"What do you think of my new granddaughter?"

Knowing that he wouldn't get a word in until they talked about Pia, Raphael shrugged. "I wouldn't be surprised if you'd custom ordered her at a store."

The old man frowned. "What? Why?"

Raphael stared into his drink. But it was the long fluid line of Pia's back, the drop of water that had run down her damp skin that he saw. The outrage in her eyes when he'd accused her. The hurt when he'd called her naive and meek.

"Raphael?" Gio prodded.

"She fits your requirements for a granddaughter a little too perfectly, don't you think?"

A sneaky smile twitched around Gio's lips. "So you admit that she is perfect."

Raphael raked his fingers through his hair, frustration and something else—no, not something else. It was lust pounding at him. Lust that had never seemed so complicated or so fierce before. And the last thing he needed was for Gio to scent how attracted he was to Pia.

"I don't mean it that way. An innocent, shy, clearly out of her depth orphan who travels across the world searching for her legacy, searching for her grandmother's lover... Damn it, Gio, you've always been desperate for a child, for someone to love. She's the perfect lure to tug at your heartstrings."

"She's nothing like my fiery Lucia—"

"Or her manipulative grandfather, if you're truly that," he added.

"*Si*. She's young and sweet. I feel as if the burden of looking after Lucia was too much for her. No wonder that man preyed on her."

Raphael scowled. "Did you even check the legitimacy of her claim before you advertised her to all of Milan with her inheritance hung around her neck like a sign?"

Gio frowned as the meaning sank in. "I have no doubt that she's Lucia's and my granddaughter."

"Excuse me if I save my teary-eyed approval for later."

"You have become a hardened ass, Raphael. Mistrustful of your own shadow."

"I'm realistic. After three marriages, one would think you would be too. One would think you'd see beneath the wide-eyed innocence and the fragile naïveté."

Silence met Raphael's outburst. A pounding was beginning behind his eyes. Something was very wrong with this talk and yet he couldn't place it.

Giovanni studied him over the rim of his wineglass. "I watched you watch her tonight. I heard some of the things you said to her. You were exceptionally cruel."

Raphael blanched at the matter-of-fact words. He had been, and that was not counting the stuff he'd said later, at the pool. He didn't like losing control of situations around him. He loathed losing control of himself. Thanks to her, both had happened tonight. And it had erased the little charm he usually had.

He'd aimed where it would hurt most and shot. He prided himself on his reputation for ruthlessness, and yet tonight it sat like acid in his mouth.

"And you didn't come to her rescue, knowing what I would do. What the hell are you playing at, Gio?"

"I knew you would grill her, that you would try to poke holes in her story. I didn't know you would dance with her, or hound her until she ran away from you. I didn't know you would lose your legendary control." He said it as if he was calculating a complex puzzle. "What did she say when you cornered her by the pool?"

A chill climbed up Raphael's spine. He'd been so close

to kissing her. If Gio had heard of it… "*Christo*, did you have the staff spying on us?"

Suddenly, the frown cleared. His eyes twinkled, in that satisfactory way that raised every hackle Raphael had. "You were more ruthless than usual. You are attracted to her…" His gruff voice deepened. "You want her." Raucous laughter burst out of him, and he slapped his thigh hard.

Raphael scowled. He had a feeling this was what Giovanni had waited and watched for. "I'd like to remind you that the woman you're talking about is your grand-daughter."

"She got behind your…defenses, isn't that what they say? And you don't like it. Tell me, Raphael, are you interested in Pia?"

Raphael sat back, something about that question sending a chill wave through him. "You talk as if she were cattle you're trying to sell," he evaded.

All he wanted to do was walk away. From this discussion and from that woman.

Of all the people in his life, Giovanni was the one person who could see through his ruthlessness, who'd known Raphael before he'd become hard and cynical. Who knew that Raphael didn't like even a bit of weakness, any trace of vulnerability. And being attracted to a woman in a way he didn't understand was a weakness.

But he couldn't leave. Not until he knew what Giovanni was up to.

"Answer the question."

"I'm rarely interested in any woman for more than one night." He made his voice harsh. "And definitely not in a woman who flees if I so much as touch her hand."

Finally, he saw a flash of his godfather's infamous temper in his eyes. His mouth lost that arrogant twist that always meant Gio was up to no good. Since he usually reserved that for his parasitic relatives or money-hungry exes, Raphael didn't much care.

"Do not cheapen her."

"I'm the one cheapening her?" He took a deep breath, modulated his tone. "Tell me, Giovanni. What does it mean if she's your granddaughter?"

"It means she already owns a piece of my heart and I will do everything in my power to do right by her. It means she inherits everything I own. Including my stock in VA."

Dio, he was going to give her the stock in VA?

The stock that Raphael wanted. He could have bought Gio out ten times over in the last few years. Could have established his exclusive ownership of the company.

For reasons he refused to share, Gio had always denied Raphael's request. Even though Raphael was the only one with executive and operational powers at Vito Automobiles, Gio refused to leave the board. In short, the old man had always loved playing games.

"So now all that stock will rest in the hands of a woman who, by her own admission, was so desperate to be loved, to be wanted, that she fell for the sweet words of a lowlife? Who not only signed away the little money she had but actually racked up a credit card debt because she couldn't bear to lose him?

"That is the woman who'll inherit your wealth? Do you know what the jackals will do to her?"

"Which is why I want to ensure her well-being. If I died tomorrow, Pia would be all alone in the world."

"And so you have advertised her to all of Milan with the size of her inheritance hanging around her neck like a bloody flashing neon sign.

By tomorrow morning, the vultures will be circling, determined to get their hands on Pia."

"I didn't advertise her, Raphael." A shadow of pain crossed Gio's usually animated features. "I celebrated her presence in my life. After years of wondering about Lucia, I finally have someone to call my own. I want to give her everything she could ever want. I want to cherish her, pamper her, protect her.

"That child is… Her innocence, there's something so fragile about her.

"Would you deny me the chance to right my wrongs? Would you deny me the pleasure of showing off my grand-daughter to the world? The chance to find a man worthy of her among the vultures?"

By sheer dint of his will, Raphael kept his shock to himself. He'd been right. Giovanni intended to buy a prince for Pia. And hand her over lock, stock and barrel. Along with his shares.

He couldn't care. He didn't.

"That's up to you. Just…don't give her any more money. Not until I confirm her claim."

"You do what you have to do, Raphael. Who knows, maybe she'll take my seat on the board?"

He wouldn't, however, watch years of his hard work being thrown away. "She's an elementary school science teacher and you want to throw her into the shark-infested pool that is the VA board? They'll pick the meat off her bones."

"She will have you to advise her and guide her."

He stood up, and put away his wineglass. "I have neither the time nor the patience to teach that woman anything. I have enough on my plate with Alyssa, with the company, and now I find out that—" he bit off the last part. Giovanni had always had a soft spot for his stepdaughter, who happened to be Raphael's ex-wife and Alyssa's mother. He didn't want Gio sticking his head in Raphael's business just as he wanted nothing to do with Pia.

"As long as you keep her away from VA, I don't care if you sign away your entire fortune to her."

Giovanni watched as his godson walked out. His breath left on a sigh of satisfaction.

By the time he was through, neither Raphael nor Pia would like him very much. But he didn't care. There was only one man to whom he would trust his granddaughter's well-being. Just as he had trusted only one man with his precious company.

CHAPTER FOUR

PIA STOOD OUTSIDE Raphael's imposing set of offices on the tenth floor of Vito Automobiles in front of his assistants' desks—apparently Raphael required two assistants—and fought the urge to turn tail and run.

She would have to run a long way though, for the stretch between the bank of elevators to the wide swath of those desks was an ocean of gleaming marble.

Stay away from me.

She cringed at the words she'd thrown at him a mere ten days ago. If only she could somehow manage a semblance of sophistication in his presence. If only her insides didn't turn to jelly the moment he was near.

But she'd never experienced anything like her attraction to him, and she didn't know how to control it.

She was still debating whether she should just cut her losses when the door to his office opened and he stepped out.

His suit jacket was gone, and he seemed to have carelessly pushed the sleeves of his white dress shirt back, revealing hair-roughened forearms and a gleaming Rolex. His hair needed a trim, and there were dark shadows under his eyes.

He was so painfully gorgeous that he took her breath away.

"Pia? How long have you been waiting?"

His frown cut through the light-headedness.

The two assistants' gazes swung to her. They shot to their feet, a torrent of Italian volleying out of their mouths.

Pia forced herself to move toward him. "I just arrived and I... I hadn't even had the chance to inquire if you were around."

He scrutinized her, from her wild hair to her summery blouse and her denim shorts—which suddenly seemed far too short—even down to her wedges, cataloging, it seemed to her, every detail before returning to meet her eyes.

There was that intensity again, that displeasure—as if there was something about her he didn't like. "Come in."

She clutched the strap of her purse tight. "It's nothing... important. Relevant even." Her idea was ridiculous. Outrageous. "I'll talk to you when you see Gio...whenever."

She hardly turned on her heel before he was there, next to her. The warm, male scent of him buckling her knees. His fingers wrapped around her bare arm sending a shocking pulse of awareness through her.

He didn't really pull her, yet Pia found herself drifting alongside him. "No interruptions," he warned the gaping assistants before closing the door.

Pia looked around his huge office, more to avoid looking at him than with real interest. A dark mahogany desk took center stage with a sitting area to one side, and a walk-through to a bedroom and walk-in shower.

She retreated to the other side of the desk while he leaned against the closed door, all casual elegance. "You should not roam by yourself in a strange country."

Some heretofore-unknown imp goaded her. "Worried about my safety?"

He rolled his eyes, which in turn made her smile. "Giovanni Vito's American granddaughter is quite the sensation right now." His gaze skimmed her face for an infinitesimally breathtaking moment. "You're a shiny target for any number of men."

He called her the vilest of things, took offense to her presence in Gio's life and yet, something in his expression made her wonder if he actually *was* worried about her.

Or maybe she was beginning to delude herself.

She sighed, helpless against the longing that, for one moment, he would see *her*. Pia. Not Giovanni's scheming granddaughter. But then, if she weren't, he'd probably not even look at her at all.

"I begged Emilio to give me a ride since he was coming into the city anyway. Gio is visiting his sister."

His gaze lingered on her mouth. Just for a fraction of a second, but there. Luckily, the desk hid her trembling legs. "Which one?"

"That mean old dragon Maria."

One brow shot up.

She colored. "She's the one who created the rift between my grandmother and Giovanni. Filled both their heads with lies. Turned their young love bitter."

He scoffed. "Don't you think *their love* should have stood against Maria's meddling? It shouldn't have sent Lucia running across the ocean and Gio to marry three different women just to mend his broken heart."

"I know what my Nonni felt each and every day of her life. And I'll… I'll thump you before I let you poison the memory of their love."

He pushed off from the door with a feline grace that sent her pulse speeding. "And Giovanni keeps assuring me that you are a sweet, too-good-to-be-true young woman who likes everyone in the world." He spoke as if her very existence was an impossibility.

Tracing the edge of the desk with her fingertip, she walked around it before he could reach her. "I usually don't hold grudges."

"Is that a warning, Pia?" he said softly behind her. She hadn't realized how close he was. "You will only let me accuse you of so many things before I become unforgivable?"

She shrugged. "My *nonna* meant everything to me. I can't forgive someone who caused her considerable harm. Which is why, while I resent your accusations, I try my best to understand your reasons for behaving as you do." She looked up and met his gaze. "You care about Gio."

Shadows filled his eyes before he nodded. "He means everything to me," he said, using her own words. "He's the one person who always believed in me. Who never asked anything of me."

The stark emotion in his voice, the honesty in his eyes—Pia shivered. This was the true Raphael. A man whom no one saw. A man, she was becoming sure, who didn't appear much. A man she respected and even liked. She cleared her throat, wishing she could shrug off the increasing connection she felt with him. "Now that we've established a common goal—"

His arm shot out to capture hers when she would have sidled away again. "If you don't stop being so nervous around me, I'll give you a real reason."

"Like what?" she goaded, pushed by his nearness.

"Are you sure you want to know?"

No, she didn't. This was dangerous. She had no business playing games with Raphael. So she sat down.

To her immense relief, he took the opposite seat. His long legs folded along the length of her own without touching. "You've been avoiding me."

"I've been avoiding the entire male population of Milan. Unsuccessfully."

His frown deepened, while his long fingers played with a paperweight. "So Gio is still determined to find a prince for his perfect princess. Tell me, is it because you've been thwarted in love that you've decided to let Gio buy you a nice, convenient husband instead?"

She stood up so fast her head whirled. "If all you're going to do is mock me, I've—"

His arm shot out and caught hers, stalling her. *"Mi dispiace, si?"*

"You can't say things with every intention of cutting me, and then expect to be let off by saying sorry. The last thing I want is to involve you. I came because I've no choice. And because, believe it or not, I trust you."

His gaze flared, caught hers, compelling and dominant. But it was she who held it, letting him know she might quiver at his touch but it didn't make her weak.

A muscle flicking under his jaw, he looked away first.

Pia felt as if she had won a minor battle. She took a drink of water and watched him over the rim of her glass.

Whatever had passed between them, it was gone. Smoothed away beneath his perfect featured mask. "Tell me why you're here."

"You were right. Giovanni hosted that ball with the intention of introducing me to eligible men. *Introducing* being a euphemism.

"I haven't had a day to myself since that blasted night. He's dragging me to party after party, brunch after brunch as if I were…a mule he's determined to be rid of." Raphael's mouth—that sensuous mouth, twitched, and Pia glared at him. "It's not funny.

"I can't turn around before there's a grandson or a son or a twice removed cousin of one of Gio's friends visiting. There's so many of them I can't even keep their names straight. If I refuse to go on an outing, Gio encourages my *escort* to walk around the estate with me. If I refuse to accompany one of them to a party, Gio takes me there anyway and then abandons me with them.

"I know and you know and the whole damned world knows that it's not my infinite charms or my breathtaking personality that brings them to me in droves. But Gio refuses to acknowledge it. Pretends as if he can't hear me when I say half of them are just plain…"

"Idiots?" Raphael offered unhelpfully.

"I've had enough of the false attention, the warm looks, the overdone praise of my nonexistent beauty. I've taken to packing a picnic lunch first thing in the morning, and escaping to remote corners of the estate to avoid them."

"No one can stop Gio when he gets an idea into his head. Why do you think he's estranged from not only three ex-wives but also his brothers and sisters?"

"He'll listen to you. He thinks you walk on water."

Raphael shook his head. "I already warned him this would happen. But he's determined to find you a…" He raised his hands palms up. The defeated gesture didn't suit him at all. "Don't shoot the messenger.

Why don't you tell him to back off?"

"Every time I bring it up, he gets all teary and senti-mental, starts rambling about the mistakes he made with Nonni and about leaving me to face men like Frank alone. He works himself into quite a temper.

"He raves about going to his grave knowing that you and I are all alone in the world. He feels responsible for you too, you know."

Raphael snorted. "You do realize that your grandfather is a manipulative bastard, *si*?"

"That's a horrible thing to say."

"Doesn't make it any less true. Giovanni will manipu-late you until you agree the sun revolves around the earth."

She rubbed her forehead, something clicking. "Wait… so you don't think I'm an impostor anymore?"

"My PI informed me that you're indeed Lucia's grand-daughter. And Giovanni's."

Which was why Raphael hadn't visited Gio. But four days and a million thoughts hadn't been enough for him to figure out how to handle the fact that Pia *was* Gio's granddaughter. Or to convince himself not to *handle her,* in any way.

There were a hundred more beautiful, more sophisticated women among his acquaintants. Women who would suit him for any kind of arrangement he wanted. Women who didn't look at him with barely hidden longing.

Women who were not his complicated godfather's innocent granddaughters.

He'd been waiting it out. Telling himself that she was just a novelty with her honest admissions and her innocent looks.

That he'd always preferred experienced women—both in bed and when dealing out of it.

And yet, from the moment he'd seen her standing outside his office, awareness had hummed in his blood.

Today, she looked the part of an elementary teacher with her black-framed geeky glasses, her brown hair in a messy knot precariously held together with a wooden stick, he realized with a grin, and a frilly, floral blouse and worn-out denim shorts that clung to her nicely rounded buttocks and displayed her mile-long legs.

With no makeup on, she should have looked ordinary. But he'd already looked past the surface. Knew that beneath the plain facade was a woman who felt everything keenly. Knew that if he touched her, she would be as responsive and ravenous as he was.

The summery blouse made her look more fragile than usual. He wanted to trace the jut of her collarbone with his fingers. And then maybe his tongue. He wanted to pull that stick in her knot so that her hair tumbled down. He wanted to slowly peel those shorts down until he found the silky skin of her thighs so that he could…

Fingers at his temple, he forced the far too vivid, half-naked image of her from his eyes. Christ, even as a hormonal teenager he hadn't indulged like that. For one thing, he'd never had a spare minute.

"You had a PI dig into my background?"

He shrugged, glad that he was sitting. "Gio has been hoodwinked by three ex-wives into not only marrying them but settling fat alimonies on them."

She got up, walked around the coffee table that separated them and sat down at the other end of the sofa he was sitting on. Tilting her chin up, she gave him a haughty look. "I'm waiting, Raphael."

He grinned. "For what?"

"An apology. What do you think?"

"Didn't you just tell me you don't want apologies for things I'm not really sorry about?"

"You're the most arrogant, annoying man I've ever met."

"Tell me what brought you here, despite that."

"Last night we had a really bad argument. He was pushing me into a corner and I... I said something really awful." Big fat tears filled up her eyes. And just like that Raphael went from mild irritation to a strange tenderness in his chest.

Raphael leaned forward and took her tightly clasped hands in his. Even as he fought it, awareness seeped through him from her hands. The rough calluses on her hands, the slender wrists, the blunt nails—everything about her enthralled him.

He looked up and his gaze snagged on her wide mouth, pinched in sadness. "What happened?"

She tugged at her hands and he let go with the utmost reluctance. "Of all the men who have been...*pursuing* me, for lack of a better word, I like Enzo the best and it was easier to spend time with him than run around trying to avoid the rest of them. I enjoy his company and we've been pretty inseparable the last two weeks. He's kind, genuine and he told me the first moment that—"

"Enzo Castillaghi?" Raphael snapped. Everything inside him came alert.

"He's gay and he told me within two minutes of meeting me. He said his family would lose it if they knew. Both Giovanni and his father, Stefano, are pushing really hard for this to go through."

Raphael jerked up straight, his blood curdling. "Stefano? He was there?"

Pia nodded, her gaze searching his. "I didn't realize Gio knew so much about my thing with Enzo. Anyway, yesterday afternoon out of the blue Enzo and Stefano arrived for lunch. After lunch, we… Enzo…proposed to me in the garden while they watched from the terrace. He said he liked me, and we could marry as a convenience for now. It would get his parents off his back and I… Gio and the unwanted attention.

Just as a stopgap measure."

Raphael cursed hard and long.

For Gio to make a deal with Enzo's father, Stefano Castillaghi, when he knew how much Raphael loathed Stefano, and with good reason… Something wasn't right. The thought of Pia married to Enzo while Stefano pulled his strings from behind, while Stefano got his hand into Vito Automobiles… His blood boiled.

What the hell kind of a game was Giovanni playing?

"Raphael, you look downright scary. Is the Castillaghi family that bad?"

Somehow, he managed to swallow the poison that swirled within. "Enzo is harmless but completely under his father's thumb. Stefano, on the other hand…"

"What about him?"

Raphael wondered if she realized she was touching him. That all he'd have to do was tilt his head and his mouth would touch hers. A thread of her scent warmed by her skin teased his nostrils. Damn Giovanni!

"What about Stefano, Raphael?"

He ran a hand through his hair. This day was going from bad to worse. "Stefano was my father's business partner for twenty years. Even as families, we were very close. As a business, my father, Stefano and the third partner made some unwise, risky investments. When the investments failed to pan out and the business went under, we found that Stefano and the other partner had cleverly claused themselves out of the debt.

My father was the only one responsible. We lost everything—our house, the business, the cars—overnight because he was determined to pay everyone back. But it wasn't enough."

"Couldn't Stefano and the other guy be held responsible by law?"

He hated talking about that time. Talking about the man he'd once hero-worshipped. Being reminded that the void his father had left had only hardened with bitterness. "No."

"You're not telling me something." Distress rang in her voice. "Your father...what happened to him?"

How could she know what he had left out? "He killed himself."

Her hands clasped his tightly, her silence saying more than words ever could. He didn't know why he held on to her fingers as if she were a lifeline. He didn't know what magic she wove but something shifted in his chest.

"Was he a good man, Raphael?" she asked in a soft voice. It was a question no one had ever asked, and it burrowed through his flesh and blood like an arrow, lodging deeply and painfully.

"He was a coward," he said harshly. And flinched, for his own words hurt him. Still. After all these years.

"You...how old were you?"

"Seventeen."

"Raphael, you don't think—"

He pushed away from her, loath to discuss his father and the past any longer. "I owe Giovanni everything but I'll be damned if I let Stefano's shadow touch Vito Automobiles. What was your answer to Enzo?"

Her gaze turned searching, and then she sighed. "I refused him. Enzo is sweet. And this offer…it will get everyone off my back, and maybe provide a measure of relief to Gio too. But marriage is sacred."

He snorted. She glared at him. "It is for me. I could no more marry Enzo as a convenience than I could marry… *you* to make Gio happy."

"There's one point in my favor over Enzo, *si*?" That she distracted him enough to joke less than a minute after thinking of Stefano Castillaghi said something about his attraction to her.

"Fat good that does me," she mumbled.

"What does that mean?" he asked, genuinely curious now. *Dio*, no woman sent him on a roller coaster as she did.

Color stole up her cheeks. "Can I finish telling you what happened?" she said tartly.

He grinned, liking her all riled up like this. *"Si."*

"After they left, Gio told me I should accept Enzo, that he would be a kind husband. When I said I had no intention of marrying in the near future, he got…agitated. I told him I'd had enough of him manipulating me. He said it was his right to select a husband for me, to make sure another man didn't cheat me like Frank did.

"We yelled at each other some more and I said if he kept pushing me like that, if he… I'd leave and never return, like Nonni had done." She rubbed a hand over her eyes, but the tears fell anyway. "His face went white…he couldn't speak. One of the staff called his physician.

"This was not like one of his usual temper tantrums, Raphael. The doctor took *ages* to get there and I thought—

God!" Her tears turned into soundless sobs and Raphael pulled her into his arms.

She came to him as if she had no strength left. Arms vined around his neck, she buried her face in his chest.

A strange sort of weight seemed to lodge in his own throat. He wasn't worried about Gio. The mean old bastard would live to a hundred and torture Raphael and Pia in the process.

No, it was the sound of Pia's wretched grief that shook him.

He had never seen anyone grieve like that. With everything of themselves poured into it. His belief that all she wanted was easy money from this trip—suddenly, his cynicism, his hard shell, felt dirty near her.

Her back was slender against his broad palm; even now he was unable to stem the awareness of her soft body against his. "Pia, nothing will happen to Gio."

"We don't know that. I can't lose him. Not when I've only just found him. To see him lying on the bed, helpless like that... All I could think of was my Nonni. I can't... I couldn't forgive myself if anything happened to him. I can't let him go on worrying about me."

"You can't marry a gay man however decent you think he is," he added softly, just to make sure they were on the same page. Right now, he couldn't even try to fathom the underpinnings of his godfather's Machiavellian mind.

She sniffled elegantly and wiped her cheeks. "No, I can't. I couldn't sleep. I was working on a toy and finally I hit on the perfect solution."

Raphael pulled her hands away from his neck because the graze of her breasts against his chest was more than he could take in his current mood.

And because, while she was obliviously dwelling on her worries over Gio, his attention had wandered from her grief, from Stefano, to the pressing weight of her thighs against his. To the span of her tiny waist and the flare of her hips in his hands. To how soft and sweet she smelled.

To the semi hard-on that was fast swelling into something else.

He only meant to create some distance between them.

But the moment she realized what he'd done, her eyes widened. Furious color rushed up her neck and she sidled off his lap as if she were on fire. Or maybe it was he who was on fire.

"I'm sorry. I didn't mean to… I just…"

Pretending a calm he didn't feel, Raphael poured a glass of water and handed it to her.

Did the woman still not realize how close he had been to kissing her again? Was she really that naive? Did she not realize her appeal, as unconventional as it was? Had the lowlife she'd mentioned shattered her confidence completely?

It was still nowhere near what Enzo with his kindness and Stefano with his schemes would do to her.

The thought shattered his desire. He couldn't let Stefano get his dirty hands on the company he had made into a global leader. But he was also running out of options.

Options that didn't involve Pia. And getting involved with Pia, his gut told him, was not a path from which he could turn back. Even if he wanted to.

He felt as if there was an invisible noose tightening around his neck.

It made his voice harsh when he said, "What is your solution, Pia?"

"You should pretend… I mean *we* should pretend to be interested in each other." When his frown morphed into a scowl, Pia hurried on. "As if we were dating each other. As if we were…violently attracted to each other and nothing else, no one else would do. It's the perfect solution," she added when he just stared at her.

"How?"

She folded her hands, realized how defensive she looked and dropped them. Did the man have to look so displeased just by the notion of them dating? "Gio thinks the world of you. If you weren't so utterly out of my league, I think he would have pushed you and me toward each other."

"What?"

"Do you need me to spell it out? It's all I've been hearing from Gio, from everyone's mouths since I arrived in Milan. About the kind of women you go for. Even Gio isn't foolish or stubborn enough to wish for something between us. Which, perversely, makes it the perfect solution."

"I have to admit your scheming does prove you have Vito blood."

"Most of the men I've met over the last few weeks, Enzo included, wouldn't dream of coming near me if you made it clear that I belonged to you. They are all in awe of the force that is Raphael Mastrantino," she added caustically.

His lips twitched. "Are you mocking my reputation?"

Pia smiled. His eyes lit up; he looked incredibly gorgeous. "I wouldn't dare."

"And you would be okay *belonging to me*?"

She shuddered. "It's archaic, but nothing else, I fear, would keep them away. This way, you can rest easy that I won't get my hands on Gio's fortune. Gio would be thrilled that I have somehow enthralled you and I... I can make plans. As much as I'm making a deal with the devil."

"I am the diablo?" he said in a soft croon that sent shivers down her spine.

"*Si*," she replied.

But Raphael was no devil. Nor Prince Charming either. He was more like the big bad wolf. But sometimes it was the wolf that provided the most protection. It was the wolf you could trust to keep others at bay.

How she would survive a fake relationship when she

couldn't even look at him without melting on the inside she didn't know. But this was the only way.

For Gio and for her own peace of mind.

He reached out to her and tilted her chin up. "What plans would those be?"

"Plans that don't concern you."

"If we start this charade, I will know everything about you, Pia."

Why did that sound like a declaration of possession? "What does it matter when you can keep me away from the till?"

Just silence. And those intense black eyes. Pia squirmed like a fish on a line.

"I... I've been thinking about staying beyond summer. Last night, seeing Gio's reaction... I realized I was just fooling myself about returning. There's nothing there for me. Not anymore.

"At the risk of confirming your worst suspicions, I want to stay here and take care of him. The thought of leaving him alone, with all his relatives who really don't care about him, leaving him with hired help, it twists my stomach."

A tightness emerged around his mouth. "Taking care of Gio, or any old man, is a full-time job, Pia."

"I know that. When Nonni was ill, it was just me and her. I took a long leave of absence and I looked after her for two years. I can—"

"How old were you?"

"Twenty. I had been working only for a few months."

"Didn't you miss having a life? The excitement of your job and friends?" His disbelief was apparent in his voice. As if he had personal experience to negate her claim.

"All we had was each other. I know Gio has you but you're always so busy."

"I see the logic in your plan. It serves both our purposes, *si*? But whether it will work, whether Gio and the world will believe that I would be *violently attracted* to such a—" he let his gaze roam over her with a thoroughness that both excited and embarrassed her "—what did you say? *Shy, plain, boring elementary science teacher,* that I'm not sure about."

In the process of tugging her bag over her shoulder, Pia stilled. Smoke should've been coming out of her ears. The gall of the man! She turned to face him, and his warm, wicked smile carving deep grooves in his cheeks, stole her indignation.

It changed him, that smile. The way he had held her when she'd cried—that was a Raphael she could like. "Just as it'll be hard for me to act as if you're God's gift to women," she said with a put-upon sigh. "But I'll do anything for Gio."

He took her hands in his and tugged, a devilish twist to his smile. "Simply liking will not be enough, *cara mia.* First, you have to stop being so nervous and jumpy around me. Then you have to act as if you adore me."

He dipped his head while locking Pia against the door with his arms on either side of her, "And then—" his breath stroked her neck while the scent of him enveloped her "—as if you can't keep your hands off me."

"No," she whispered, her entire body languorous as if someone had replaced the blood in her veins with warm honey.

A feral smile curved his mouth. "*Si.* Didn't the gossip mill tell you the last bit about me?"

Pia couldn't move her gaze from his mouth. The defined upper lip and the lush lower lip. No man should have lips like that. The need to taste that sensual mouth, the need to press her body against those hard muscles was like a physical ache. How could she feel an attraction this strongly when it was one-sided?

"That you never have a girlfriend, only lovers," she

forced herself to say, remembering the tidbit. And yet, apparently, it didn't put off most of the women.

"If we have to make the entirety of Milan believe that we're together, I can't be seeing other women on the side, *si*? So it'll be up to you to keep me in—"

Pia slapped her palm over his mouth, a thrill running through her.

If she wanted to live in Italy, if she wanted to be a part of Gio's life, it meant Raphael would forever be a part of it too, in some way.

Was she forever going to spend it shying away from him? Twisting inside out because of her attraction to him? Letting him mock her like this?

Something within her rebelled, made her say, "Maybe it won't be so bad pretending to be your girlfriend."

His eyes widened. "I realized something about Frank and me in the last few days. He singled me out for his attentions for a reason. I… I wouldn't have been taken in by his sweet words if I'd had more experience with men, *si*? Both emotionally and…sexually." It was one thing to want to take down his arrogance a notch, and completely another to do it with his mouth against her palm, his stubble scraping her fingers.

He wrapped his fingers around her wrist and tugged it back, his face so close to hers now that she could see the slight widening of his pupils, the flare of his nostrils. He wasn't just playing with her, something whispered at the back of her mind.

"Even I didn't realize how perfect we are for this pretense. It's clear that I'm not the type of woman who could interest you in a million years." The sound of his choking laugh made her glare at him "And… I could never have a relationship with a man like you."

"Non?"

"No. You're arrogant, cynical and…far too gorgeous for

me. I'd have to beat off women for the rest of my life. I'd be reminded every day how fortunate I was to have you. Things would always be unequal between us. Love or not, I'm determined not to be with a man who looks down on me, who thinks he's doing me a favor by being with me."

A faint flush appeared under his cheekbones. "Pia, whatever that lowlife said—"

"Let's not forget the whole you despising marriage thing," Pia cut in, refusing to let him finish. The last thing she needed was Raphael's pity.

"You still want to marry?"

"Of course I do. I refuse to let Frank break my beliefs that've been a part of me much longer." Though he had come pretty close. "My parents, from what I remember of them, were devoted to each other. I want a man who'll respect our relationship, a man who'll trust me, a man who wants to spend his life with me. And in the meantime, I can hone myself on you, can't I?"

"What would this…*honing yourself on me* entail exactly?" He made the words sound so utterly debauched, so wickedly filthy that Pia could feel heat burning up her neck.

Turning the handle behind her, she slipped out without answering. But his laughter, a deep, sexy sound, a sound that rendered his assistants awestruck, a sound that sent tingles up her spine, stayed with her all the way through the ride home.

Making her wonder what she'd signed up for.

CHAPTER FIVE

Dress for me tonight.

RAPHAEL'S TEXT THAT very evening, just as she had been getting ready to leave with Gio, mere hours after they'd made their deal, stopped Pia in her tracks.

Dinner at his sister's house. It was the perfect occasion to advertise their new relationship. She could just imagine the arrogant gleam in his eyes, the roguish curve of his mouth as if he were standing in front of her.

That's how Gio caught her, standing in the hallway, looking at her phone, first baffled, then furious and then with a goofy smile on her face. Because the arrogant Italian would've known how much it would rile her to get that command from him.

And he couldn't have orchestrated it any better if he had stood there and kissed her.

When Gio had inquired who had made her smile, Pia had instinctively ducked the phone behind her. Realizing Gio was exactly why she'd begun this, she'd reluctantly shown him the phone.

Her grandfather had stared at the phone for a long while. Which had caused her to wonder if she'd made a horrible mistake. When he had finally looked at her, Pia had expected a hundred questions, meddling, plans. Gio, she'd begun to realize, could be like a little boy sometimes—temperamental, impulsive.

But Gio had said nothing. Asked nothing.

She'd have thought he didn't approve if he hadn't uttered, "He is a good man, but hard. Do not let him break you like I broke Lucia, *si*?"

He'd been worried at her revelation, but on the drive to Raphael's sister's house, Pia had sensed Gio's relief too. Almost as if he had known this would happen.

As if it was what he'd wanted.

The growing unease that she'd started something that had no exit strategy only deepened as Pia smiled at, shook hands with and exchanged air-kisses with a crowd of curious, but mostly friendly faces as soon as they arrived at his sister Teresa's house—a posh Mediterranean-style villa with colorful ivy climbing decoratively up its white walls.

Golden sunlight washed over the villa. The early dinner was al fresco with people spread all over the house and the immense backyard with white tables spread around. A festive atmosphere reigned with kids chasing each other and people talking in groups. But the moment Gio and she had walked in, a hush fell over the smiling faces.

She tried not to cringe as attention focused on her. More than a few faces were familiar, even a couple of men who had attended her ball. Suddenly, her plan sounded ridiculous, even stupid.

She was going to pretend to be familiar with Raphael in front of all these people? Pretend like just the thought of being romantically involved with him didn't make her feel plain and dull? Didn't make her want to hide and do something wildly exciting at the same time.

And where was the dratted man anyway?

Pia met Raphael's four sisters and their husbands, scores of his nieces and nephews—they were a fertile bunch, apparently—a host of his cousins and their spouses, two aunts, one uncle and finally his mother Portia Mastrantino.

That same distrust she'd seen in Raphael's eyes showed in his mother's eyes.

Noting the white shorts and skirts paired with spaghetti tops and the humidity that was making her hair wild, she was glad that she'd dressed in a plain cotton navy blue top and printed shorts with her favorite Toms wedges, whatever Raphael's imperious command.

After more than an hour of blank smiling, Pia sneaked into the house, needing quiet.

Sitting on a chaise longue in cargo shorts and a navy blue T-shirt that exposed corded arms and hair-sprinkled wrists, Raphael looked utterly different and yet just as magnetic. Floor-to-ceiling glass dipped him in sunlight. His olive skin looked darker, his shoulders broader with the fabric stretched over his lean chest.

He was bouncing the most adorable little girl on his knee.

The little girl screamed and laughed as Raphael pretended to lose his grip on her while she slid down his long legs to the floor. Every time he caught her at the last second, she squealed, shuddered, scampered over to his knee, climbed over his chest and wrapped chubby arms around his neck and slobbered a wet kiss over his cheek.

Again and again, he pretended to lose her, she did it all over, planting another wet kiss over his other cheek. His dark eyes roared with laughter, love, eagerly awaiting the moment when she would kiss him.

A pulse of longing reverberated through Pia at the sight. Such cynicism when he addressed Pia and now for this girl, such affection.

Was she a niece? A cousin's daughter?

Suddenly, the little girl hiccuped. Her chubby face scrunched tight. Holding her as if she were the most precious thing to him, Raphael asked for a glass of water. Three dark-haired voluptuous women rushed to his aid, all of them dressed in the latest designer clothes—thanks to Gio, Pia now had a useless font of information about couture.

The women hovered over Raphael anxiously, ready to do his bidding. To his credit, Raphael had eyes only for the little girl. He didn't notice the adoring glances or how each woman found a way to sidle closer to him or touch him in some way.

Hot embarrassment poured through Pia. Followed by a thread of sheer possessiveness that rocked her.

Was that how she watched him too? With that barely hidden longing and her attraction plastered all over her face?

Worst of all was the sinking awareness that she was nowhere near the league of the women that hovered around him like bees around honey.

Something about Raphael, even as she disliked his cynicism, made her body sing, made her mind weave impossible fantasies.

She couldn't forget that Raphael had agreed to their pretense for his own benefit. And not because he saw her as a woman worth his interest.

Feeling something prickling at the back of his neck, Raphael looked up amidst Alyssa's slobbering kiss on his cheek.

Pia stood at the center of the room, her eyes wide behind a pair of black-framed spectacles. Sunlight drew an outline of her lithe body in a simple T-shirt and shorts that bared her long, tanned legs. She'd braided her hair but was losing the fight against it. It fell in unruly curls around her face.

Among the women dressed in casual couture with designer handbags and diamonds dripping at their ears and wrists, she stood out like a wildflower amidst pricey, carefully cultivated crossbred prize orchids.

No makeup, no artifice.

Emotions chased across her face, the naked vulnerability in it rousing desire and a fierce protectiveness within him.

Pretending a liaison with her, however harmless she thought it, wouldn't be without consequences. His conversation with her at his office, Gio's Machiavellian maneuvering of them both toward what he deemed inevitable, every instinct Raphael possessed told him that it was a bad idea, screamed at him to keep his distance from her.

And yet, how could he leave her to the jackals Giovanni had unleashed on her? To Gio's ridiculous schemes? The thought of any man, even Enzo, touching her, the thought of her bestowing her friendship, her loyalty, her affection on any other man—it was becoming unbearable.

Was she going to fare any better with him? The question had been haunting him since he'd agreed to her scheme.

"Pia?" he whispered softly.

She lifted those luminous eyes to his. A jolt of sensation hit his muscles at the artless want in her eyes. Her open desire for him made every male instinct in him rise to the surface.

Color washed up her cheeks and she blinked. "I was looking for you," she finally said, pushing the glasses up on the bridge of her nose. "I don't think we should—"

He could see Giovanni and his mother and a couple of other people walking into the huge room. "Come and meet my daughter, Alyssa." He cut her off abruptly.

"Your daughter?" She looked like a deer caught in headlights, ready to flee any moment. "You have a daughter?"

His daughter slid off his legs, sauntered over to Pia, wrapped herself around Pia's bare leg like a vine and looked up. The thought of Pia's dislike for him translating itself to Alyssa made him cover the distance between them.

All her distress forgotten, Pia picked up Alyssa with a soft laugh. Raphael watched transfixed as she buried her face in Alyssa's tummy with a sigh.

He could hear Gio in the background saying what a pretty picture the three of them made, the manipulative bastard! Could imagine his mother's shock; could practically hear the wheels turning in her head; could hear the soft whispers spreading from mouth to mouth.

Raphael had never believed in fate or higher power. None of them had ever come to his aid. Always it had been his own decisions and actions that had made his path. Even after Giovanni had taken him under his wing, it was Raphael who'd pushed himself to set new goals, to reach new heights in his business.

And yet, as Alyssa twisted one of Pia's curls around her chubby finger and tugged hard, sending a gush of pained tears to Pia's eyes and laughter spilling from her mouth, it felt as if he was taking a step that couldn't be undone.

He laughed at the way Pia cooed at the three-year-old in fractured Italian, begging her to let go of her hair; at the way she instantly dropped to her knees when Alyssa demanded to be set down and tugged Pia in that boisterous way of hers.

Amused, he watched as his daughter and Pia charmed each other for the next hour. He watched his daughter, who barely tolerated strangers, instinctively trust Pia, and he watched as Pia, who'd been so uncomfortable with the sophisticated crowd, fell for his girl.

Slowly, Alyssa began to sway where she stood. Pia gathered Alyssa—who didn't let anyone except him or his mother put her to sleep—and she neatly cuddled into Pia's chest, sucked her thumb into her mouth and promptly fell asleep.

"Don't wake her up," Pia hissed at him when he tried to untangle her hair from his daughter's fist.

Only this woman could make him laugh just as much as she could turn him on with one look. "Unless you want her to rip out your—" his gaze fell to the thick honey-brown strands that were like rough silk between his fingers "—lovely hair, which would be a shame, I have to do this." Firmly, he uncurled Alyssa's fingers until Pia's hair was free. "Believe me, she has ripped out my hair from the roots far too many times."

"You don't look like you've lost any," she threw back, and then blushed when he grinned. He took Alyssa from her, gave her to his sister, who left with a wide-eyed glance at the both of them.

Having lost their buffer, Pia stepped back from him hurriedly. She frowned as she noted Gio and his mother in deep discussion outside the French windows. "You didn't tell me you have a daughter."

"Alyssa is no one's business but mine," he said before he could modulate his tone.

Hurt flashed in her eyes before she lifted her chin in defiance. "Is your ex-wife here too? I'm not really comfortable stepping in between—"

"Allegra is not a part of our lives anymore. She lost all her rights to Alyssa."

"I wouldn't have suggested this ridiculous charade if I'd known you had a daughter. I won't be a part of anything that could harm that little girl. Maybe she's too young to understand which woman her father is…has…"

He raised a brow.

She was the first woman who hadn't immediately thought to use Alyssa like a ladder toward him. The first woman in his sphere who had considered his child's interests before her own.

She was the first woman he'd ever met who *always*

put someone else before her own needs—first her Nonni, Gio and now a little girl. Even his mother, who adored her grandchildren, sometimes used Alyssa to try to manipulate him.

But Pia... Could Pia be truly different in this too?

"Do you always stammer when you talk about what men and women do?" he goaded.

"It can't be good for her to know you and I...you and me..."

"My mother and my sister Teresa are the only ones who're allowed to look after Alyssa," he offered. He'd never explained his actions to anyone and yet the words fell from his mouth. "I need a woman for only one thing and I do that when I'm out of town."

"You need a woman for only..." Her words trailed off, a flush dusting her cheeks. "That's horrible and so...clinical. Are you saying you'll never need a woman, even in the future, for anything else?"

"I'm saying exactly that. I don't intend to marry ever again."

"What about affection, companionship, y'know..."

"I've never met a woman who made me feel or want those things. Alyssa has me, and my mother and sisters for a woman's influence." He took a step toward her, more turned on by this ridiculous conversation than made sense. The infuriating woman took another step back. "My mother will understand that our relationship is not something I want discussed in front of Alyssa. She wasn't even supposed to bring Alyssa today. But I bet she couldn't pass up the chance to meet you."

"When I met her...she..." Pia hesitated. When he just stared back at her, she finally said, "I could be wrong, but I think she...doesn't like me."

"She doesn't."

"Why? She doesn't even know me."

"You're the prime contender for Gio's fortune."

"That's a horrible thing to say," Pia said laughingly. But the seriousness in Raphael's gaze sobered her up. "How do I know you don't feel the same? Do you see your piece of the pie getting smaller? Maybe *you're* the one manipulating *me*?"

He laughed, as if the very idea was ridiculous.

The confidence he wore like a second skin—that didn't come without bending life to one's will. Giovanni had told her how Raphael had taken VA public, made gains they hadn't seen in the last decade. He'd been ruthless about the changes he'd enforced, wasn't the least bit sentimental about what needed to be done, but his execution was always effective, she'd been told by her grandfather, curiously with something like regret in his eyes.

More profits. Better stock prices. He had no friends he trusted, no one was indispensable to him. No weakness was allowed in himself or tolerated in others.

The shadow of his father's suicide, Pia realized now, would forever cast a black shadow on Raphael's life, and would never let him be anything but a man who loathed weakness.

"If you're wealthy, then why would your mother worry?" she countered.

He shrugged, but Pia could see it bothered him by the tightness of his mouth. "She grew up in a very wealthy family and my father kept her in the same style. When we lost the house and our lifestyle, a lot of her friends and connections turned their backs on her. She took it very hard—wouldn't leave her bedroom, refused to eat. She became a ghost."

"It couldn't have been harder on her than it had been on your father, could it?" Pia was unable to keep the sarcasm out of her voice.

She waited for a cutting comeback. He simply frowned.

"I'm sorry, that was unkind. It's just that…your father was betrayed by people he trusted. People with whom he shared his fears and dreams and hopes. Your mother still had him and you and your sisters. What's a fortune when you have family and friends who love you?"

"You really believe that, don't you?"

Pia shrugged, uncomfortable with his scrutiny. "I just… I can imagine what your father must have felt. What Frank did to me is minuscule by comparison, and yet I have days where I can't trust my own judgment. Days when I can't believe that everything he did was with a motive—pulling me from the dark cloud of Nonni's death, persuading me to step out of the house for an evening.

"Gio didn't help by doing what he did either. I can't trust anyone—man or woman—when they say something nice to me. I can't help but search for deeper motives. Perversely, it's what makes me trust you."

His frown only deepened. "What about me?"

"Your animosity, your suspicions. I can count on you to be brutally honest, even if I don't like your assumptions. The reason why I…" *like you.* She cut herself off at the flare in his eyes. Words solidified the feeling in her chest. The last thing he needed was to learn that he was beginning to grow on her. "I don't understand why your mother doesn't like me still."

"She lives in a permanently terrified state that I will take the same risks with my money that my father did and doom them all. She made sure I allocated lifelong separate funds for my sisters, for Alyssa and her."

"Funds you cannot invest in your business?" Pia asked, shocked by the implications. It not only showed a distinct lack of faith in Raphael's abilities as a businessman but also a callous obsession with wealth over her son's feelings.

"*Si.* Over the last few years, she got used to hearing Gio's continual claims that he will leave everything to me—which he did to annoy his ex-wives and their constant bickering for more settlements. It has turned into her insurance against my possible failure and downfall. Now you are a threat to that insurance."

Was it any wonder he assumed she was out to fleece Gio with the mindset he already had?

To believe that one's own mother saw one as nothing but a source of her income… Could Raphael see himself as anything but a provider? Had he even been allowed to grieve for his father before he'd had to take on the mantle of his family?

Because, despite everything, it was clear he cared about his family. She had called him ruthless, but not enough to stop shouldering the responsibility of his sisters and their families.

And he adored his daughter.

Suddenly, Pia saw Raphael more clearly than she ever wanted to. She didn't want to see any depth to his hardness, any soft edges beyond his cynicism. She didn't want to see Raphael as anything but an impossible fantasy and a reluctant ally.

She didn't, couldn't afford to see him as a man worth knowing.

CHAPTER SIX

WIDE EYES DRESSED with the longest lashes searched and studied his face unblinkingly as Raphael waited. Dappled in the sunlight, she looked exquisitely innocent. Desire was a permanent drumbeat in his blood anytime he was near Pia. But it wasn't just that anymore.

She had a way of looking at him that made him feel bare. Of making him speak of things he'd never mentioned to anyone. Of looking deep beneath his words and showing him a side of himself he'd never seen before.

The shame of his father's suicide was a wound that had festered for too long. And yet, beneath it, he recognized the pain of betrayal he hadn't seen until now.

He had worshipped his father and overnight, his hero had both abandoned and betrayed him. But in memory, his father had lingered on in what he had felt then was the epitome of weakness.

"Take care, Pia," he whispered. Until now, he'd let Gio coerce him. But the feeling of losing control made him snarly. "Is it any wonder Giovanni wants you tied up to some man as protection? You stare at me as if you mean to gobble me up."

"Not any man, just you," she replied, and then blushed furiously. "It's good to know that you care about your daughter."

Instead of mollifying him, her apparent approval riled

him. Damn it, the woman turned him inside out. "Because you assume I'm an uncaring monster?"

Another step forward by him and another backward by her. "All indications said so."

"Stop backing away." The comment hissed out of him in a low growl.

"Stop crowding me. Stop…" A panicked gasp fell from her mouth. "This is a bad idea on so many levels."

Every time he came near, he could see the pulse fluttering madly in her neck. See her breaths hitch in and out. Feel warmth arc between them.

But despite the attraction, he was beginning to believe she wanted nothing to do with him. The thought rankled.

He'd never been vain, but no woman had ever *resented* his attentions. Not since he had become taller and broader than any boy he had known in his teens. Not since he had remade his family's fortune ten times over. Not since he'd become one of the most powerful men in Milan. "What is a bad idea?" he asked, closing the distance between them once again.

"Why would Gio involve Enzo and Stefano even indirectly if he knew how much you loathed him? You were right, he…"

"Manipulated us, *si*," Raphael finished for her.

It burned Raphael that Gio would use Stefano to rope him in, but Pia was right. Unless Raphael did something to calm Gio down, his schemes would only get wilder. No measure would be unacceptable if Gio thought he was doing it for their good.

If he thought it would push Raphael into taking Pia off his hands.

"Then you know why we can't—"

"Let Gio think he's been successful. Let the whole world think you've beguiled me," said Raphael.

"How do you think I feel knowing that he went through

this elaborate charade to...*coerce* you into this with me? As if I were useless inventory he wanted to move? As if I were a pawn to entice the mighty King?"

"He's manipulative, *si*, but it doesn't mean he's not worried."

Shaking her head, she backed away. "But I don't like—"

Before she could utter another word, Raphael caught her upper arms, tugged her toward him. "I told you what I would do if you did that," he said with a growl before he touched his lips to hers in a soft buss.

He only meant to shock her, he told himself. To show her that being attracted to him wasn't the end of the world. That her idea was indeed the perfect solution for now.

Except all his reasons flew away the minute her mouth stilled under his.

Her hands caught on his chest. The long lashes cast crescent shadows on her cheeks. But it was her wide eyes that snagged Raphael. The slumberous desire in them. The soft mewl of pleasure that fell from her mouth as her palms moved and settled over his chest. His heart thundered like a wild beast under her palms, her body's warmth slowly infiltrating his.

One kiss... All he wanted was one kiss.

One taste of the tantalizing lushness of her mouth. One taste to see if she was as sweet as she sounded.

One moment with the woman who stared at him like no other did. As if he were her deepest fantasy.

"Raphael..." Her entreaty incensed him. How dare she walk into his domain and turn him upside down?

Fingers curled around her nape, he tilted her face and slid his tongue over her trembling lower lip.

She moaned into his mouth—a tremulous whimper that heated his blood. And shuddered. Her body softened and his hardened. Fitting his mouth flush against hers, he moved it this way and that. Heat stirred from that soft friction and her fingers became stiff against his chest. Digging and pressing. Grasping.

He kissed her mouth again and again, a soft slide, a hard press, teasing and taunting, somehow controlling the feral hunger blooming in his blood. "Open your mouth, *tesoro*," he pleaded, every muscle curling in heated anticipation.

Her body arched into his touch even as she said, "They're watching…please…"

And yet, she pressed closer, until her small breasts were plastered against his chest. Until her thigh was encased between his own. He stroked his hands up and down her back, soothing those infinite tremors, willing her to take the leap. Mindless hunger consumed him. "Give in, *bella*. Kiss me."

And merciful God above, she did.

Slowly. Softly.

Like a whisper of a butterfly's wing, she pressed a tentative kiss at the corner of his mouth, flicked his lower lip with the tip of her tongue. From one corner of his mouth to the other, she kept kissing him until it felt like there was a hot poker inside of his own body. Until the control he was exercising spewed hot shivers all through him.

Again and again, standing on her toes, sinking her hands into his hair, pulling him down… All he'd done was touch a spark to dry tinder and she'd exploded. His body's hunger deepened. His need deepened.

With a growl, Raphael stopped her explorations. Holding her still, he plunged his tongue into her mouth, again and again, the kiss turning instantly carnal. He licked the warm cavern of her mouth, curled the tip of his tongue against hers, begging her with his caresses.

He was pleading her for surrender, for he instinctively knew only sweet entreaty would do with Pia. She wasn't delicate inside, only outwardly. That sweet innocence of her spirit, he would do anything to keep it intact.

Shuddering, she returned the pressure, her tongue touching his in tentative strokes. His moan imploded, reverberated through his own body as the kiss grew urgent. He kissed her hard and fast, his need only increasing the more he took. Sweet and hot, she was like a drug he'd never known.

Christo, she was responsive, ravenous as he was.

He dug his teeth into her lower lip and tugged. She whimpered. The sound was so soft, so much of submission and surrender.

His erection, already incredibly hard, lengthened against the cushion of her soft thigh. Flipping them, he held her against the wall, pulled her leg up until it was wrapped around his hip. Groaning at the indescribable sensation, he cupped her behind with his hands and pressed her against him tighter. Rocked himself into her groin gently.

Pleasure balled at the base of his spine, warmth seeping through her clothes to touch his skin. God, he wanted to be inside her before he took another breath; he wanted to move inside her while she stared at him with those wide eyes...

There was the sound of a cough, a whispered snarl from Gio. Raphael backed away as if burned. A curse flew from his mouth. His breath burned in his lungs, his body raging to finish what they'd started.

Dio mio, when had he been so aroused from just a kiss? With his daughter in the other room, with his mother and sisters and half of bloody Milan watching? When had his hunger ever betrayed him like that?

Breathing hard, he counted to ten, his erection no less painful at the end.

Eyes big in her gamine face, Pia remained flat against the wall where he'd pinned her with his body. Hair wild from his fingers, mouth bruised from his kisses, eyes wide.

A fierce satisfaction filled him to see the marks of his passion on her. To see her— He cursed again.

Damn it, this wasn't one of his sophisticated lovers who knew the rules. This wasn't a woman who wanted Raphael for one quick screw or even a short affair. By her own admission, she didn't even know her own sexuality, as explosive as it was.

She looked so bewildered and so innocently seductive that it doused the heat running through his veins and replaced it with a strange unsettling feeling. As if he'd opened a door to something much more complex than a kiss.

"Pia?"

She ran a tentative finger over her lower lip and a groan vibrated in his chest. "I feel…as if…" She wrapped a trembling hand around her nape, moved it forward over her neck, placed her palm over her heart. "My heart is thundering. Frank never kissed me like that. No, he tried. It just never felt like that. As if I were sinking and flying at the same time."

He fisted his hands, her words balling into pleasure at the base of his spine.

"Why did you stop?"

Christo! That was the question she asked? "Because I was this close to taking you against the wall. And I heard Gio—"

"Taking me…" Her gaze took in his balled fists, the muscle jumping under his jaw, moved to his groin and noted the evidence… "Oh." Liquid longing peered out of her gaze.

He closed the door with a slam on prying ears, his temper getting the better of him. "Don't look at me like that."

"Look at you like what?" Slowly she pushed up from the wall, a faint tremble to her movements. The passion cleared from her face, her jaw lifting in that stubborn way.

"Why are you looking at me *like that*? As if I've done something wrong?"

"It was just a kiss, Pia." It hadn't been just a kiss. In thirty-four years, he had never lost his mind like that. He'd never wanted to take a woman against a wall, propriety be damned. He'd never been so desperate to protect and possess someone as if his breath depended on it.

"Was it? Because it feels—"

"*Si*, it was just a kiss." He bit out the words so forcefully she flinched. "A show for Gio and my mother and all of Milan." Ignoring her pale face, he continued on, the ruthless bastard that he was. "I have kissed a hundred women just like that and done a lot more besides. It's lust, nothing more, nothing to be upset about. Nothing to weave dreams about.

"Just because you react like dynamite to a spark when I touch you, it doesn't mean we would suit," he added for good measure.

Color fled her cheeks and he fisted his hands. *Could he do or say nothing right with this woman?*

Christo, this was Gio's precious granddaughter. Touching her when he had no intention of going any further, kissing her when he knew she was innocent, but even more than that, there was something about Pia that got under his skin, that lingered long after she was gone.

There was something about her that made Raphael want, something in her gaze when she looked at him—as if she could see more than what he was: a ruthless, hardened cynic.

How dare he kiss her, then act affronted because she liked it? Dear God, she could still feel the sharp pulses between her legs. Could feel his warm breath on her cheek, his fingers on her buttocks.

That kiss had been such pure pleasure that she couldn't

feel the ground now. And yet, Raphael seemed determined to flatten her with reality.

A show? Who was he kidding?

"We're both responsible for that kiss turning into something else," she said, her voice vibrating with hurt and anger.

"Sì."

"Then you're unhappy because I enjoyed it more than you think I should?"

"I lost control. And it won't happen again."

"The kiss or losing control?" Pia demanded, her heart already taking a beating. How could she forget the impression of the hard column of flesh that he'd pressed against her belly? Had that been part of the pretense too? When he opened his mouth, she held him off. "Stop talking before you say something I can't forgive."

Eyes flaring, he looked away. In profile, his face was tight with control. His impressive chest rose and fell.

"Are you all right?"

"No. I'm not all right." She wished she could lie, but what was the point? Just as she couldn't become beautiful or sophisticated, she couldn't play games either.

Oh, why had she involved him in this farce in the first place? She'd thought she'd somehow resist her attraction to him, but she hadn't counted on finding such a complicated man beneath. He was tying her up in knots—and that was when he wasn't kissing her. "I don't kiss a man as if my life depends on it, and then coolly wipe it from my mind."

When he reached for her hands, Pia shied them away. A tic beat violently under his jaw.

He didn't want to have kissed her, yet he didn't like it if she turned away from his touch. What did he want from her?

"You have to. I won't let it spiral like that, but if we have to keep this pretense up some intimacy will be required."

Understanding dampened the scorching trails his body had left across hers. This was how he usually had his affairs. Except she hadn't followed the script. "I can't just separate it like you do. I can't turn it off when it's inconvenient."

His eyes flared. "Convenient? Nothing about my life has been convenient since you decided to storm into it. First, he had all of Milan tripping over themselves to get to you. Then, he puts you in my way by involving the damned Castillaghis in this whole thing. Do I worry about the threats my ex is making about Alyssa or do I worry about which man's trap you'll fall into next? My whole life has been turned upside down because of your presence. Damn Gio and damn…"

Pia flinched at the vehemence in his words. Did he really resent her presence in his life so much? Tears prickled at the back of her eyes and she shut them away.

Perhaps sensing how she'd retreated from him, he took a deep breath, ran a hand over his eyes. Whatever he claimed, it was clear that the kiss hadn't left him unaffected.

He reached her and traced a finger against her jawline. The tenderness in the gesture stole her breath just as much as the kiss had done. Made her long for something that he clearly wasn't going to give. "You kiss me like you can't stop, you snarl at me for turning your life upside down, and then you touch me as if I'm precious. I don't understand you, Raphael."

"How is it that a smart science teacher can't figure out cause and effect?"

"Cause and effect?" she repeated stupidly, blinking up at him.

"No good can come of this. I will never marry again, much less love again. And you, even after what that man did, you still have stars in your eyes. I kiss you because I can't help it." A ragged growl punctured his words. "I kiss you because everything about you drives me crazy. All I can think of when I wake up or go to bed or when I take myself in hand is how good it would be to move inside you. How good it feels when you come alive in my arms. But all I want from a woman is one night, a short, torrid affair at best. You're not offering that, are you?"

She shook her head automatically, and he snorted. "I didn't think so."

With one searing glance at her mouth, he walked away, leaving Pia quaking as if she'd been through an earthquake.

An affair with Raphael—even one night with him—letting his strong body cover hers, welcoming that hardness into her body, letting him see her at her most vulnerable… Heat flushed from every pore. Her body trembled just at the images, hungered for what she knew would be unbearable pleasure.

But it was her heart, drumming even now, that she was afraid of.

Frank had only chipped it. Raphael, given a chance, would crush it.

CHAPTER SEVEN

ANY DOUBTS PIA had about Raphael's promise were proved unnecessary over the next few weeks. Any momentary, crazy belief she might have had in his matter-of-fact statement that he wanted her despite his legendary will, shredded in the freezingly polite way he treated her.

Forget kissing. He didn't even touch her unless it was for an audience. Even then, he barely held her arm with the tips of his fingers as if she would contaminate him. Even his accusations had felt more personal than this.

The news that Raphael Mastrantino was dating Giovanni Vito's granddaughter swept through society faster than the heat wave that had descended on Milan.

If Pia had thought she'd garnered too much attention as Gio's American granddaughter, it was nothing compared to the glances and whispers thrown her way as the woman who'd caught Raphael's interest. His public possessiveness had fended off any other man's interest, exactly as she'd intended.

Giovanni, while he said he was delighted with this turn of events, was strangely toned down.

Pia, however, hadn't foreseen how torturous their little facade would be to her. Or that the more she saw of Raphael, the more she found a man worth admiring.

He was the perfect son, the perfect brother, the perfect boss, although a little distant, if all the things Pia had heard at an office party were to be believed. From Gio, she knew he was the perfect godson. As one woman had explained in lurid detail at another party, unaware that Pia stood behind her, he was a perfect lover.

No, scratch that, the woman had been aware that Pia was there and had taken a petty satisfaction in making sure Pia overheard.

In front of Milan and Gio and his family, he was the attentive boyfriend or lover or whatever the hell it was that they were pretending to be. Every day, he sent her flowers or candy or some other treat. When she'd asked if he'd bought her a subscription for a gift club for the next few years, he'd snarled something in Italian.

She'd had her answer, which festered. She was nothing but a painful chore for him, an item on his damned to-do list.

Between a huge deal VA was cooking with a manufacturing company in Japan and his time with Alyssa, he was hardly available anyway. Their pretense was barely a blip in his life. Whereas for Pia, every carefully orchestrated touch was torture. Every moment she spent in his company, she was caught between wanting to run away and desperately wanting more.

As if that wasn't enough, Raphael came to see Gio most evenings. Sometimes, it was a quick chat under Gio's watchful eye.

Sometimes, they dined outside with the spectacular view of the setting sun drawing pink and orange mirages on the lake. If there was enough light or if Gio petulantly demanded that he hadn't seen enough of them together that week, Pia joined them. She brought out a piece of wood and worked on it quietly while listening to Raphael relay the news and politics of Vito Automobiles.

He spoke with a deep, confident voice, his Italian soothing to her ears. Even though she only understood a few phrases, Pia heard his passion for his work, his affection for Gio in the way he relayed tidbits about people they both knew.

She could just sit there and listen to his voice endlessly.

Pretending that all the hours she spent in his company gave her rights over him, while pretty much every woman snidely commented that it was the Vito Heiress that had snared him, grated like salt on a wound. As if she didn't know that Raphael wouldn't have looked at her twice if not for the fact that she was Gio's granddaughter.

On one such scheduled outing, she'd persuaded Raphael to bring Alyssa along. She adored that little girl, and to her shame, Pia desperately needed a buffer—there was only so much one-on-one she could take with Raphael before she did something crazy.

Raphael had returned after a week-long trip and any hopes she'd had that she would be over him were dashed to tiny bits when she saw him striding up the pathway with a squirming Alyssa on his shoulder and his mouth stretched in carefree laughter.

They spent the next two hours with Alyssa at a *gelateria* in Menaggio, another one of the picturesque villages lining up Lake Como. Pia held a chubby, sticky and sleepy Alyssa in her arms while Raphael parked the car in front of his mother's house.

When he asked to take her back, Pia shook her head, loving the feel and weight of the little girl. Despite her mother's absence in her life, Alyssa was such a darling little girl that Pia couldn't help but fall in love with her.

And every time she was with Raphael and Alyssa, Pia couldn't fight the rightness of it. Couldn't fight the longing that drowned her. As if she were the piece of the puzzle that he and the little girl were missing.

But it was ridiculous. Even if he asked her, she didn't want to be with a man like Raphael, did she? Ruthless, rigid...

Raphael leveled the strangest look back at her.

"Show me the way," Pia said in a husky voice. Only when she followed him down a quiet corridor did she realize that the house was empty and her only buffer was snoring slightly.

"I'll get her into her pj's," she said to Raphael.

Again, that intense, almost searing look.

"You can trust me with her, Raphael," she burst out, a tight knot in her throat. "I adore her."

His mouth tightened, as if she'd threatened his very safety. "My mother should have been here. She knew I had plans tonight."

"You don't want me in Alyssa's life," she said, busying herself by looking through the drawers for clean pj's. It wasn't personal, she told herself. But it was a lie.

She wanted things personal between them. She wanted him to tell her private things, things he never confided in anyone. She wanted him to tell her what his ex had done that he didn't trust any woman anymore.

She wanted their facade to be true. She wanted to be the woman that Raphael forsook any other woman for, that Raphael broke all his rules for.

"I get that. Believe me, I do. I think you're a wonderful father. She won't wake up. And you can go call your mom while I settle her down."

Instead of reassuring him, her words made him look even more forbidding. With a short stiff nod, he walked out of the room.

By the time, Pia had cleaned up and changed Alyssa, the sun was beginning to set. Making a face, she pulled her damp T-shirt off her chest.

The moment she walked into the outer lounge, Raphael stood up. His gaze took in her wet T-shirt. He scowled. "You should have called me when she woke up."

"She didn't. I had some trouble working those monstrous taps at the tub and splashed myself." It was the first time they had been alone since that episode at his sister's house. Pia wiped her damp hands on her jeans, butterflies partying in her stomach. "Didn't you have an engagement to get to? I can stay until your mother comes back."

"Teresa will be here any minute. Then I will drop you off and continue to my engagement."

Pia nodded, unease climbing up her spine. It was the way he said it. It was the way he wouldn't meet her eyes.

"Who are you meeting?" she asked. She tried for nonchalance but wasn't successful.

"It's an old friend who's in town. We have a standing engagement when she's here. I completely forgot about it. But since she's here—"

Pia's heart sank to her toes. "She? It's a woman?"

"Si."

"Is she single?"

"Si."

It was like getting blood out of stone.

"So this engagement is sort of a date?"

His silence told Pia everything she needed to know.

Walk away, a part of her screamed. *Turn your back on this, on him,* came another warning.

But dear God, she'd make herself crazy imagining all kinds of scenarios. "If it's a date, won't she talk about it later? You know, to someone who knows Gio? Wait, doesn't she know that you…you're supposed to be engaged?"

"I'm sure she's heard the gossip now."

"And yet, she called you?"

He pushed his hand through his hair roughly, his gaze never leaving hers. A sense of dread curled up in Pia's stomach. What was he saying that she wasn't understanding? God, how she loathed her lack of sophistication.

Instead of answering her, he dialed Emilio on his cell

phone, ordered him to pick up Pia, and then hung up. "It's getting late. You should be getting home."

"I don't get it. How can she want to go on a date if you're in a relationship?"

With me, she left out the pathetic lie that she was beginning to wish was true.

"It's not that kind of a date. Ava and I know each other from university. We're friends and—"

"Lovers?" She had no idea how she'd been able to say it without choking.

Their gazes collided and held, a hundred unsaid words flying in between. Finally, he nodded.

Everything fell into place. "So you're going there to just…" Heat climbed up her face. "You're going there to have sex with her?" she forced herself to say, images of him kissing some faceless woman bombarding her.

"Ava and I go way back and I just… I need to be anything but your lover right now."

Anger came to her rescue. The thought of Raphael with another woman made bile rise to her throat. "Are you that heartless?"

"Heartless?" A tightness crawled up his face, making him that arrogant stranger from the ball. "You've begun to believe your own lie, *cara mia*. I don't remember promising you anything, much less my fidelity. You mean nothing to me, Pia. You need to remember that you and I wouldn't have crossed paths if not for the fact that you're his granddaughter. *His precious princess.* And the cost of touching you is…far too high for me."

Each calculated word landed like a poisoned arrow. God, how could he hurt her like this? Why was she letting him?

She had had enough of this pathetic spectacle she was making of herself. Enough of wondering if he would ever look at her with something other than polite courtesy.

"Brutally honest, as ever. At least you're reliable. But you know what? I can't do this anymore. I—"

"You can't do what?"

"I can't pretend to be your bloody girlfriend. Frank was right. I'm not sophisticated enough for these kinds of… Find a way to call this thing off. Find a way to protect your bloody company from Giovanni's meddling. But I'm done with this, with you."

She turned and angrily swiped at her cheeks. Damn it, she refused to cry in front of him. His pity would kill her.

But she got no more than a few steps before he slammed his palm on the door. She couldn't turn. She couldn't bear to look at him anymore. "I don't understand you at all. Foolishly, I thought I was beginning to. That you were more than the ruthless, ambitious businessman that everybody calls you. What you're thinking, it's horrible, clinical."

The warmth of his body, the scent of him seeped into her back. One more step and she would be in his embrace. Oh, how she wanted to take that step, how she wanted to lose herself in him…

"You, this pretense, it's driving me crazy, don't you get it? I'm wound up so tight I can't sleep. I can't work. You're—" But she cut him off before he could say the horrid words.

"I'm ruining your life—yes, I know," she said loudly, tears knotting in her throat. "You think it's easy for me? The whispers I hear, the snide innuendoes, that the only reason you're with me is because of what Gio has. That Gio's wealth compensates for what I lack.

"It's like reliving the episode with Frank. Only, this time, I know the truth beforehand."

"Damn it, I'll knock the bastard's teeth down if I see him ever."

"Just tell me one thing. Were you lying the other day

at your sister's house? Were you just protecting me and my tender feelings? Was it the fact that you haven't been with anyone recently that made you lose control? Tell me that being with another woman while you want me doesn't bother you, and my rose-tinted glasses will come off."

Raphael couldn't answer her. He couldn't say no. It didn't matter that even the very idea of touching Ava felt like a betrayal of his own self.

Damn it, even his overnight trip to Venice, his meeting with an old friend, which should have progressed from the restaurant to her hotel room, it had taken all his wits just to get through the dinner.

All he could see in the woman who'd been a friend for years was the brittleness her two divorces had given her, the false warmth of her smile as she'd played footsie with Raphael's leg under the table, the utter lack of connection between them.

Because of the infuriating woman and her outdated ideas about affection and companionship and respect, all his old connections began to look cheap and tawdry.

She was turning his life upside down.

He owed her nothing. He needed her to see the true him. He needed her to realize that he was no hero and definitely not hers.

And yet, the words wouldn't rise to his lips.

All he could see were her big eyes that saw too much. Her lush lips. Her chest falling and rising. The raw honesty of her emotions was written across her face. So was the desire that she couldn't hide every time she looked at him. And the ease with which she was fitting into his very life. Her adoration of his child...

The remembered taste of her was a siren's call he couldn't resist. Without warning, he suddenly kissed her. Hard and hungry with not a bit of his usual finesse. He devoured her mouth with bites and licks and nips until she was moaning and arching into his touch.

"This is what you want, Pia?" he said, pulling her skirt up. Sending his hand on a foray for silky skin, even as he plunged his tongue into her sweet mouth and swallowed her yes.

How he wanted her now, here. He wanted to thrust into her wet warmth and get rid of this madness.

What magic had she woven around him?

He cupped a barely covered buttock with one hand while his other met the soft, sensitive skin of her inner thighs. Mouths tangled, he pushed aside the silky thong she wore until he could find her core.

Sweat dampened his brow. A current of electric desire pooled in his groin as he found her soft folds.

Dio mio, she was ready for him. Silky and slick against his fingers.

He swallowed her soft gasp, pressed her against the door. Pulled her leg up until she was wide-open for him.

Without giving her a moment to breathe, he set a fast rhythm with his fingers. She sobbed, she moaned, she was like a spark plug touched by the fire.

Madness filling his blood, Raphael snaked his tongue around hers and increased the pressure of his strokes.

The moment he rubbed her swollen clit in concentric circles, she broke apart. Her spasms against his fingers sent his own blood rushing south. Her soft cries pelted against his skin.

He wanted to push her hair from her damp forehead. He wanted to take her in a soft kiss. He wanted to tell her she was incredibly beautiful, that her passion would bring any man to his knees.

He did nothing of the sort.

If anything, tonight only proved how wrong they were

for each other. How dangerous she was to his control. How easily he could break her spirit.

He pushed away from her. Like the ruthless bastard that he was, he didn't even try to hold her up when her knees shook beneath her. Her eyes were closed; her face was turned away.

But he didn't miss the lone tear that tracked a path down her cheek.

"That is all I can give you, Pia. That is all I give any woman."

He walked out of that room and the house and went outside to wait for Emilio.

CHAPTER EIGHT

"How DARE YOU go behind my back after everything I've done for you?"

Raphael refused to look up before he finished perusing the design document as Giovanni walked into his office with all the force of a stomping elephant. The rush of affection welling up in his chest was a soothing balm against the guilt festering for the actions he'd taken.

Giovanni meant the world to him.

He had taught Raphael to aspire to bigger dreams, had spotted Raphael's unusual talent for fixing cars of any kind, believed in his talent and hard work when even his mother hadn't.

He'd been expecting this siege for a week now. From the minute he'd set about buying more and more stock in the company. Getting the members to oust Gio from the board—whose proxy had rested with Raphael all this time anyway.

If he succeeded, Gio wouldn't ever be able to bring someone like Stefano onto the board. He'd never be able to manipulate Raphael again. He'd never put Raphael in a situation where he had to face Pia again.

But of course Gio had his spies in the company just as Raphael had his at Gio's house.

Once he finished, he closed down the design software and leaned back in his seat.

"Good afternoon to you too, Giovanni," he said casually, and only then looked up to meet his gaze.

A thread of unease wrapped itself around his chest, tugging hard.

His eighty-four-year-old godfather had the stubbornness of a mule and the constitution of a boxer. And yet, his pallor was visible under the olive of his skin. Concern pushed Raphael out of his chair as Gio huffed into his office with short breaths and irately dismissed his chauffeur Emilio.

Who cast a worried glance at Raphael.

"You look like hell, Giovanni." Try as he might, he couldn't stop the concern seeping through. Emotion was a weakness that Gio would lap up.

Giovanni walked into the sitting area, his body vibrating with his famous temper. "I look like hell because my godson—the boy I taught everything—is a backstabbing cheat." A string of Italian fell from his mouth as Gio detailed all the *backstabbing* Raphael had done.

However pale he might look, Raphael didn't intend to go on the defensive. "Have you no explanation for why you are trying to push me out of my own company?"

"I'm cleaning house. I should've done it years ago."

"You're the bloody CEO, Raphael. What more could you want?"

"You and I are both aware that a quarter of the board members are always looking for ways to go behind my back. I'll not tolerate any dissent. This is my company now, Gio."

"No one would dare question your command. They know it's you who drives the stock prices higher. Your reputation is fierce. And if they crawl back to me, it's because they know you loathe them."

"I loathe them because they're not worthy of anything." Half of them had turned his father away during the hour of his need. "I'll not allow any vipers on the board."

He was deceived by the very people he trusted.

Pia's words wouldn't leave Raphael alone. In eighteen years, he'd not once looked at it that way. He'd only seen his father's actions from the perspective of a seventeen-year-old boy. But never as a man who'd been betrayed, as a man who'd been honorable until his last breath.

"Your work consumes you." He sighed. "I think at the cost of everything else. This compulsion you have to reach even higher goals…"

"It is what keeps my family in the style they're used to."

"*Si*, exactly. This wealth, retrieving your family's social standing, it's an obsession. Marco wouldn't have wanted you to sacrifice your personal happiness."

Hands clenching into fists, Raphael turned away. "I'm nothing like my father."

Gio's head jerked toward him as if Raphael had committed blasphemy. "Businesses fail, Raphael. Men make unwise investments, bad choices."

His throat raw, Raphael gave voice to the pain he had bottled for years, the complaint he hadn't let himself make even in the darkest of his nights. "He took the coward's way out. He should have been a stronger man." *For me.* Shame choked those two words.

"He adored your mother—did you know that? He spent years building his little business, trying to win her hand. But at the first sign of calamity, Portia fell apart. She blamed him. Your mother's inability to cope with the loss, the weight of your sisters' disappointments, the large unit of leeches that constitute your various uncles and aunts and cousins, and their taunts—that was what sent him to that early grave. No one believed in him anymore, Raphael, not even the woman he loved."

Raphael felt winded as if he'd been dealt a hard blow. He'd thought of his father as a coward. Instead, had his heart simply been broken? Had he given up on them because they had given up on him? Because he couldn't bear to be diminished in the eyes of the woman he loved?

His father had been a man who'd cared deeply, a man who'd loved his wife, his family from the bottom of his heart.

His vulnerability had only brought him ruin and a broken heart. "You backed me into a corner. And I fought back."

A shrewd light entered his grandfather's eyes. "How?"

"You'd hear it from my own mouth? About Pia?"

He shrugged and examined his nails. "What does my granddaughter have to do with you buying up stock?"

"*Basta!* Stefano Castillaghi, Gio? You think I'd let that bastard touch VA? Did you think I'd ever give you the chance to pull something like this again?"

"So you claimed Pia." A cat wouldn't have looked as satisfied as Gio did. That his hunch had been right made Raphael's blood boil.

"I didn't claim Pia as much as I agreed to her scheme about pretending that I did. You terrified her with your demands and your ill health. She came to me as a last resort."

Silence thundered in the air instead of the outrage he'd expected. Damn it, had Gio known that it was a pretense too?

"No one will come near her again. At least no one that cares about her and not her wealth. In the last month, all of Milan has seen how possessive you are of her. Do not think I have not seen you look at her like a starved dog stares at meat."

"*Christo*, Giovanni. Do not be crude. That is your granddaughter you speak of."

"See how protective you get of her? You might as well see the pretense through and marry her, Raphael. You want the company? It's yours. You want my share of stock that would rightfully be hers? It's yours. All I ask is that you take care of her. You watch over her when I'm gone. Marry her, Raphael."

All his bluster had been leading to this. Every move he'd made since the night of the ball had been toward this. "You know I'll never marry again."

"Pia is different from Allegra, from any other woman you've known."

"She's not my type," he said, even as the idea took root, digging into him and settling down. He forced a harshness into his voice. "She's neither beautiful nor sophisticated. She wears her heart on her sleeve. She sees too much where there's nothing."

He hadn't thought of her as anything less than intoxicating for so long. He was always on edge because his only satisfaction came from his imagination and his hand, while seeing Pia every day. While touching Pia. While her subtle perfume and body heat sneaked into his bloodstream.

Worse was the bruised look in her eyes after what he'd done at his mother's house. She barely even met his eyes anymore.

Gone was the laughter, the teasing wit, the endless questions about his past, his mother and sisters, and even Alyssa.

With one ruthless move, he'd shattered her rose-tinted glasses but he hadn't realized how much it would disturb him that he'd become less in her eyes too. He'd thought it was better to alienate her but it had backfired. And he hated himself for what he'd done to her.

"A girl with more substance than glitter is not your type, *si*." Giovanni snorted with that proud wisdom that the old thought they had over the young.

Raphael could not say it was not justified. This one time.

He had gone for the glitter once before, had come away burned. Allegra was all polished veneer with no strength beneath. His mother had once been called the beauty of Milan. She was not cruel or fickle like his Allegra had been. She even loved him and his sisters, in her own way. But Gio was right, she possessed nothing of substance. She had had nothing to offer his father when he'd needed her the most.

And Pia was as different from his mother or Allegra as he himself was from his father. He would never trust anyone like his father had done. He would never need a woman's strength like Marco had done. He just didn't have that kind of vulnerability.

Would it be so bad though?

Giovanni, sensing victory, went in for the kill shot. "You're a fool if you don't see that I offer everything you want, Raphael." He stood up, and again, Raphael was hit with how old and frail—no, how ill Gio looked. "But I'll not have you chasing her away."

Shock hounded away concern. Damn it, his priorities were all skewed. "What are you talking about?"

"She's talking of returning to the States for a short trip. That she…whatever it is, it's because of you. You owe me this, Raphael. You owe me the peace I would get knowing that Pia is safe in your hands. Before—"

Raphael never got a chance to reply, for Giovanni collapsed midway through the sentence. Heart jumping into his throat, Raphael barely caught him before Gio hit the ground.

And while he watched the paramedics carry Gio out, Raphael knew everything had changed. With his attraction to Pia getting out of hand every single day, with Giovanni's mad schemes spilling over into his health, with the sharks that would forever circle Pia whatever measure he took, there was only one solution.

His fate was sealed and so was Pia's and he would be the one to make the stars fall from her eyes.

Because he could never give her what she wanted, and now he would be preventing her from finding it with anyone else.

CHAPTER NINE

RAPHAEL'S APARTMENT WAS located in a trendy, upscale area of Milan's fashion district. The lights and fanfare of the canal district were visible from the tenth-floor apartment. Yet there was utter privacy too.

After the harrowing week at the hospital with Gio, the quiet and the ultraluxury didn't sit well with Pia. Both of them had spent the whole week in the hospital, keeping a silent vigil by the side of the man they adored.

She hadn't argued when he had commanded that she would rest at his apartment for the night.

They both knew she needed the break. At least they'd learned that the heart attack had been a mild one, and that Gio's diet was the primary culprit.

She poured herself a glass of Chianti from the wine rack and walked through the open, contemporary plan. She wished Raphael had stayed but he'd barely showed her to a room before he'd made his escape.

Maybe he was afraid she'd pounce on him again.

A harsh laugh escaped her as she remembered asking him if he was also afraid that she was stealing his share from Gio's wealth. Clearly, Raphael had his own fortune to manage and didn't need Gio's. She explored the steel and chrome kitchen, the state-of-the-art gym, two balconies, a humongous study with a dark mahogany table in the center with a picture of Alyssa and floor-to-ceiling bookshelves with mostly books on automobiles and engineering, a sitting room and two guest bedrooms.

She took a long shower in the attached bathroom of the guest room, only realizing then that she didn't have any fresh clothes. Delving into the closet provided a white dress shirt, pressed and folded and a couple of packages of women's new underwear. The bra was two sizes two big. Trying hard to rein in her riotous curiosity, Pia donned the underwear and the shirt which fell to her thighs. And knew it was Raphael's.

Instant comfort surrounded her at the faint scent of him. But it was unbearable too. Because nothing had changed.

She still wanted him. And not just for a quick screw, as he had called it. Even with things awkward between them, she couldn't help but soak in the warmth and strength of his presence over the last week.

Efficient and ruthless as ever, he'd chased away the hordes of Gio's relatives that had descended on the hospital with one look. When one had called him a backstabber, Raphael had simply shrugged it away.

He'd been fierce, as if he could hold Gio to this earth by the sheer force of his will. He had let her borrow his strength, his conviction. He'd even made her smile when he'd snarled that the old goat was far from done manipulating the pair of them.

But Pia knew him now. She saw what no one else did under that ruthless exterior. Gio's attack had shaken him. She could feel something eating away at him, not that he would talk about it. And least of all with her.

He'd made it perfectly clear he wanted nothing to do with her.

As she sank into a deep slumber, Pia could think of no other man she'd want by her side protecting her.

No man she wanted to know more. No man she wanted to risk her heart with.

* * *

Raphael had just finished his quickly put together 2:00 a.m. dinner, and poured himself a glass of red wine when he heard soft steps behind him.

Dannazione, he had tried not to wake her...

Closing his eyes, he stayed where he was, with his back to her. But he could see her reflected in the glass panes in front of him.

Clad in his white shirt, which fell tantalizingly to her thighs, she was rubbing sleep-mussed eyes behind him. He should have trusted his instincts and stayed at the hospital.

But he'd given his answer to Gio tonight and the knowledge of it was like the continual strike of a spark plug to fuel.

"Raphael?" Her husky voice floated toward him across the kitchen.

Swallowing the last of his wine as if it were water, he turned.

Her hair created a vaguely golden halo around her face, her long, long legs—toned and nicely tanned, bare from her thighs down—hit him hard. All these days, he had watched her, wanted her, with a desire that grew stronger by the minute. He'd held off because he had no intention of taking her when he didn't want a relationship. No intention of being roped into anything he didn't want.

Now there was nothing to hold him back. Nothing to stop him from possessing her.

"Sorry I disturbed you. Go back to sleep," he said, not quite meeting her eyes.

She shook her head and a mass of hair fell forward. It was an utterly feminine gesture he was sure she didn't even realize she'd made. He kept the marble island between them, as if physical distance could somehow negate the hot pounding of blood in his veins.

"I had already woken up. For a few minutes, I couldn't

remember where and why." She rubbed her eyes with the back of her hand.

That she felt so comfortable with him to stand in his apartment in the middle of the night, half-dressed, when she'd always been like a skittish horse around him, it denoted a level of trust he'd never wanted. "And then I had this sick, twisted feeling in my tummy. I thought I had lost Gio and you were... Then it all came crashing down and I jerked awake."

She leaned back against the wall, which made the shirt pull up. Another inch of toned thigh was displayed and his body tightened another notch. Her pose made those small high breasts of hers jut forward.

Alluring and sexy and like a gift for him to unwrap. He swallowed hard.

He needed to go to bed and so did she. Separately. And yet he couldn't help asking, "I did what in your ghastly nightmare, Pia? What could be so much worse than walking away when you were trembling from the orgasm I gave you?"

"You were screaming at me that it was all my fault. That I... I killed Gio."

Reaching her, careful not to touch her, he said, "You've had a strenuous week."

She dragged her fingers over her face, leaving impressions, "Oh, God, what are we going to do?"

"We're just going to sleep for about forty-eight hours." The image of sleeping with her—their limbs tangled, her lithe body pressed against hers—hit him with a fierce longing.

"I couldn't sleep with all these thoughts swirling in my head. Would you tell me the truth if I asked you, Raphael?"

He instantly became wary. "If I can," he said reluctantly.

He'd always been the protective type with his sisters and even with Allegra. After everything she'd done, it was he who had finally dragged her to the rehabilitation program. Whether he believed she'd get through it was a different matter.

But with Pia, he was aware of all of his shortcomings. It was as if she constantly held up a mirror for him and he couldn't bear to see what it would show. He didn't want to hurt her. He didn't want to do anything that would break her pure spirit.

He couldn't stay away from her either. Not anymore. Suddenly, he felt as if he could breathe again.

"Did I cause Gio's attack?"

"Pia—"

"No, please. You don't know. But I…a few hours before the attack, I told him I wanted to…to take a trip."

He stayed silent, not trusting himself to pour out the whole terrible argument he'd had with Gio.

He had been pushed and shoved to this step by Gio, by circumstance, even unknowingly by Pia, but he wasn't going to doom their relationship from the beginning.

Pia, he knew, didn't give two hoots about VA or the stock or Gio's fortune. The last thing she needed was to know what Gio had offered Raphael.

"I wanted to get away for a while. I thought I could go back to the States and tie up some loose ends. I told him it was just temporary—"

"Because you wanted to avoid me after what I did?" This more than anything angered him. "Did you think of how Gio felt at that? Do you always run away if it gets hard, Pia? Isn't that what you did when that man cheated you?"

She paled as if he'd struck below the belt. She tilted her chin in that stubborn way of hers. "I wasn't running away. I needed a break. It was hard to be around you knowing that every minute you spent with me was under sufferance."

"That's—"

"Please, no lies. The one thing I know I'll always have from you is honesty. Don't take that away from me now. You can barely stand to look at me when we're together." Pain flashed through her eyes, the raw intensity of it skewering Raphael where he stood. "You… I forced you to give me what you didn't want to. I clearly can't take a message."

"*Dio mio!* Is that what you think? When will you understand that—?"

"You've made it clear that I'm nothing but another millstone of responsibility around your neck. Another person who's dependent on you, another duty you perform even though you resent the hell out of it.

"I'm not angry with you. I see all the responsibilities you shoulder, how seriously you take them. I just can't bear to be one of them. I don't know how to make Gio believe that I can look after myself."

He reached her and ran a finger over her jaw. She had such soft skin and he wondered if she was like that all over. "And what if saying no to you was the hardest thing I ever did. That even if you hadn't waylaid me, I wouldn't have been able to go through with it with… Ava. That every time I close my eyes, I feel that velvety, swollen center of yours between my fingers. That every time I hear your voice, it reminds me of your soft moans and throaty cries. That every morning, I wake up with an erection and that I get myself off like an uncouth teenager by picturing you bare and writhing beneath me, begging me to take you." She stared at him with such wide eyes, such naked lust that Raphael was tempted to take her right there.

He brought her hand to his abdomen and then down below where his hard-on was throbbing painfully. "I can't breathe your scent without getting hard like this. Do you believe me now, *tesoro*?"

Liquid longing filled her eyes. She bent her forehead to his shoulder and breathed hard while her hand shaped him.

Raphael buried his face in her hair, something more than lust driving him. Tenderness, he realized. He wanted this. He wanted her. And not just for one night or for a short affair, as he'd thrown at her cheaply. The thought of Pia ever sharing this intimacy with any other man drove him out of his mind.

She was his, whether she knew it right now or not. "For the first time in my life, I want to be selfish. I want to take you for myself and damn the consequences. You don't know how many times I had to remind myself that you're my godfather's granddaughter."

Pia stepped back, heart pounding a hundred times a second. She could still feel the shape of him in her palm, could feel the tension radiate from him. Stark and etched with want of her, only for her, he was the most beautiful man she'd ever known. "But I'm not just his granddaughter. I'm *Pia*, Raphael. And I wish—"

He covered her mouth with his palm and pulled her to him. "Pia, look at me. Listen to me, *cara mia*." Roughly, he pushed his hand through his hair. "Sophistication or beauty or whatever you think you lack—none of the women I know could hold a candle to you." A frustrated hiss left his mouth. "It is exactly why it's hard to take you."

The words came so simply, so easily then. "But you're not taking, Raphael. I'm giving myself. Isn't that my decision?"

A hard curse fell from his mouth, harsh in the silence. Clasping her cheeks, Raphael swooped his mouth down on hers.

Hard. Hungry. Hot.

Thumb on her chin, he pressed and Pia opened with a deep groan that reverberated through every nerve ending.

She'd been dreaming of this fevered desire between them, of seeing that dark glitter in his eyes, of the handsome, gorgeous, sophisticated Raphael wanting her beyond any other woman.

All the reasons she shouldn't be desperately clinging to him were reduced to ashes. All the misgivings and doubts she'd harbored about feeling so much for him evaporated into mist by the heat between them. The rasp of his hair-roughened wrists under her palms, the rapid beat of his pulse against her skin, short-circuited her last rational thought.

His thumbs pressing oh, so firmly against the corners of her mouth, again and again, he dipped his mouth over hers, never resting, never fully giving her what she wanted.

On the next dip, he swiped the seam of her lips with his tongue and Pia melted into his body. Her hands rose to his shoulders, pleading with her touch. Wrapped around his nape, conveying her need for more, she sank blissfully into the rough swathe of his hair, an intimacy she'd been craving for so long.

A fine tremor ran through his body. "Let me taste you, *cara mia*. Let me show you how much I want this, no, how much I *need* you."

Pia opened her mouth under his, his words lighting a fire in her very blood.

The taste of him exploded in her mouth. Her lips stung when he rubbed his against hers and then cooled them off with a lick. His teeth sank into the cushion of her lower mouth, sending sharp arrows of pleasure down her body, and then he soothed the hurt with a puff of air.

Again and again, he plunged his tongue inside her mouth, a silky slide against her own, an erotic invitation to play with him one moment, a divine promise the next.

"Raphael, I…oh, please," she sobbed when he pulled his mouth away from hers.

Tall and arrogant, he stared down at her with glittering

eyes. His nostrils flared, his customarily mocking mouth swollen lush.

She would have dropped to the floor like a puddle of feelings if his hands hadn't anchored her. Even there, his hold was less tender and more aggressively possessive.

A sharp laugh fell from his mouth. "I can give no sweet words. I will make no promises, Pia. Do you still want me?"

CHAPTER TEN

KNEES SHAKING, PIA drank him in. His black shirt unbuttoned to his chest, jeans hung low on his hips, he was a dark fantasy come to life. His rough hair stood up, thanks to her fingers, but it was his penetrating stare that took her breath away.

The depth of desire in it singed her skin.

His gaze was more questioning and combative than anything her imagination could have conjured.

But this was Raphael, so ruthless and yet so tender at times. There was nothing sweet and romantic about him. Nothing sensitive and cajoling about him.

His gaze swept over the naked length of her legs, the pulse skittering wildly at her neck. Her sex clenched, hard and sudden, at the masculine possessiveness written across every inch of his proud face. "No words, *cara mia*?"

And the truth of him as he stood there, as he stared at her with absolute desire etched into taut features, darkening those deep-seated eyes was more real, more telling than any sweet words he could have given her. She hadn't felt a millionth of this wonder, this ever-present thrum before.

Months with Frank couldn't measure up to a moment with Raphael.

"I know you, Raphael, and I want you," she said simply.

With rigid movements that spoke of his control, he picked her up.

Pia wrapped her hands around his neck, touching the

base of his head with the tips of her fingers. Every inch of him was a pleasure point to her seeking, searching fingers.

She hid her face in his chest. Heat from his skin filtered through his shirt, and warmed her cheek. The thundering beat of his heart matched hers and calmed something inside of her.

Her breath fled her body afresh when he crossed into his bedroom to Raphael's vast bed and laid her down. Dark gray sheets and curtains made the room utterly masculine. His gaze drinking her in, he pulled his shirt off in one smooth movement.

The strong column of his throat and the width of his shoulders made her chest rise and fall. Taut, gleaming olive skin stretched tight over lean musculature greeted her. Sparse hair covered his defined chest, arrowing down over his abdomen and disappearing into his jeans.

Low-slung, those pants revealed narrow, defined hips.

But it was the front of his pants, showing unmistakable evidence of his desire, that caught Pia's rabid attention. His shape and size was clearly identifiable even like that.

A rush of wetness slid between the folds of her sex. Pia crossed and uncrossed her legs, a restless slithering in her skin as she heard his rough exhale.

"What does looking at me do to you?"

She jerked her head up. Heat built in her chest and began flowing up her neck and cheeks. His fingers fluttered over the waistband of his jeans and intense curiosity thrummed in her blood.

She was about to work up the courage to touch him when he spread her legs shamefully wide and stepped between them. The naked glory of his chest muted any words Pia was capable of uttering.

With a hard pressure, Raphael pulled at the base of her neck. "What happened when you looked at my arousal,

Pia?" He breathed the question into the crook where her neck met her shoulder.

Wrapping her hands around his midriff, she hid her face in his chest again. Everything she was feeling, everything he said, this moment so thick with desire, it was such a profusion of sensations like she had never imagined. "Please, Raphael... I can't speak it. I can't..."

With a hard laugh that sent shivers down her spine, he took her mouth in a ravishing kiss that plundered beyond just her lips. It was as if with every kiss, he was stealing away parts of her.

Pulling away from the languorous weight of his kiss, she tilted his head down so she could look at his face. His lips were swollen this time. His nostrils flared, his jaw so rigid that Pia caressed it tenderly.

She drank him in, from the small scar on his upper lip to the small mole near his eyebrow.

"I'm sorry I... I can't give words to what I feel. I..."

"Nessuno." A forbidding look descended in his eyes. "Never be sorry for what you are, Pia. Not with me. Never with me. I forbid it."

His thunderous expression made her smile. His arrogance that he could just forbid her from feeling stuff! "But I heard that men like women to be adventurous in bed." She loved being with him in this moment. The promise of their near-naked bodies was heady, her desire for him thrilling. But it was the peek inside of Raphael's head, this insight she was getting into the core of the man that Pia relished the most.

His fingers gripped the collared edges of her shirt, "I do not care what you heard or were told, Pia. Your diffidence only makes me realize how much you must want to let me do this."

She frowned. "Do what, Raphael?"

The ripping of the buttons on her shirt was the answer to her question.

She gasped at the coldness of his palms as they cupped her small breasts. He pushed her and she bowed back, her trust in him complete. His mouth buried between her breasts, Raphael punctuated his kisses with words. "What I want from you, what will pleasure me, I will teach you, *si*?"

"I want to please you," she whispered softly.

His eyes flared hotter. "You will." Pursing his mouth, he nipped her flesh, leaving a wet trail. "And what will pleasure you, what will send you over the edge, we will discover it together."

"*Si*," she said, floating on a cloud of sensation and never wanting to come down.

In return for her surrender—or was it reward?—he separated the edges of the shirt and pushed it off her shoulders. It hung at her elbows, baring her to his drinking eyes.

They darkened impossibly as he stared at her small breasts with their plump nipples painfully distended.

No man had ever seen her like that and Pia couldn't bear the potency of the moment, of things that she hadn't even considered. Of things she had already given over to Raphael by giving him this intimacy.

He pressed a reverent kiss to her midriff, his large hands easily spanning her waist, then a trail of hot, wet kisses up and down, from her navel to her pubic bone.

The cool sheets were a welcome contrast against her burning skin as he busied his fingers with her breasts.

He licked the aching tips as if he were testing their rigidness, their plumpness. Soft flicks, long, leisurely flicks, his gaze telling her without words how much he liked the taste of her. Gauging with those piercing eyes what she liked.

Pia arched her chest into his mouth, pressed her fingers into his nape to keep his mouth at her breast, and then flushed at her own shameless abandon. Eyes dark, Raphael noted it. She closed her eyes.

Every sensation was magnified a million times. A running kaleidoscope of colors burst behind her closed lids, as if her every sense was on the verge of explosion, of new birth.

The rough, sucking sounds he made with his lips, the Italian that emerged from his mouth drove Pia wilder, hotter, wetter between her thighs.

And suddenly his mouth was gone, leaving her desolate. Her eyes flew open, her breath serrated.

His eyes gleamed with possessive wickedness, a feral satisfaction. "I wish I could show your face to you now, *mia cara*. Your eyes are so wide that they drown your face, your mouth is pink and swollen from my kisses, your skin is trembling and marred already with my attentions…

"Shall I carry you to the mirror, Pia?" His eyes held hers, a thousand unsaid desires in them, dark fantasies she could see them both drowning in. There would be nothing of her that he didn't touch, that he didn't take. Nothing he didn't own. "Shall I show you what I see? How beautiful you are?"

She opened her eyes, saw his nostrils flare. And blushed hot when she sensed the scent of her arousal thick in the air. A muscled leg thrown over her thighs, he leaned over on an elbow.

"There is nothing shameful about what you feel for me, *tesoro*. About what you need from me." His mouth closed over the turgid nipple and pulled, and Pia jerked. She clutched her thighs tight as sensations zoomed and coalesced there. As if there was a direct connection between her nipples and the shockingly wet place between her thighs.

His broad palm descended between her thighs and when

Pia squeezed them again under another pull of his wicked mouth over her nipple, he was there, giving her the pressure she craved.

His fingers opened her up, a wicked smile curving his lips. Holding her gaze captive, his sculpted mouth blew on her hot, wet nipple, and his fingers drew mesmerizing circles over her folds, stroking, petting, spreading the dampness.

And then his finger was inside her, stretching her.

Spine bucking off the bed, Pia gasped at the sudden invasion.

"You've never done this before?" he asked softly, as if he was afraid to scare her off.

Pia couldn't even answer, for every ounce of her brain's rationale was busy processing the caresses of his thumb. Somehow, dear God, he'd found that spot that seemed like her entire being was centered there even as he pumped in and out with his other fingers.

Pressure drew her body tight, like a bow stretched too much. "I would like an answer, *mia bella*."

Pia shook her head frantically chasing the speed she needed, arching her lower body into his hand. "No. *Per favore*, Raphael…"

"Anything you want, *bella*."

And then his thumb settled there, pressing and stroking mindlessly until Pia writhed against that touch, frantic in her own skin.

It was science, it was hundreds of years of evolution and yet what Raphael did to her felt like magic. As if what happened between them couldn't be explained away by a theory.

The world dissolved into pure sensation as he stroked her just the way her body needed it. Unbearable pleasure broke over her in cresting waves, building one over the other, throwing her out into the space and then gathering her back into herself, but a different version. And when she fell back to the ground, Raphael was there to catch her with his warmth, his endearments and praises, with his arms.

Desperate to keep touching him, desperate to keep the connection even as those powerful tremors in her lower belly ebbed, Pia pushed back a lock of hair that had fallen forward onto his forehead. Realizing the possessiveness of the action, she stilled.

"Touch me, *bella*. Anywhere you want."

With a sigh, Pia greedily ran her fingers over his taut form.

He prowled over her on all fours and she reveled in the feral hunger stamped over every tight muscle, every jutting bone. She wanted to shatter his control. She wanted him as delirious with pleasure and need as she was. She slid her questing fingers over the rough silk of his bare back, loving the grooved line of his spine. He smiled against her neck, interrupting the kiss he'd been pressing there.

Dark eyes held hers captive, a stark honesty to them. "You wear everything on your face, you tell me in beautiful, honest words what I do to you, your body sings for me when I so much as brush the tip of my finger against it…" Slowly, as if he were a jungle cat, he shed his pants and boxers.

How had he known what she had needed to hear? How did he know that she wanted to please him, if it was the last thing she ever did?

He brought his body down over hers until they were flush from shoulder to thigh to foot.

Pia grasped his back with both hands, drowning in a surfeit of sensations—his angular hips cradling hers, muscular thighs pushing her into the bed, his hands kneading hips and cupping her buttocks. "Do you see how desperately I need you?"

In reply, she slid her hands to his hips. Hard muscles,

velvet rough skin, hair-sprinkled limbs so different from her own and yet so perfectly complementary and then there was a litany of Italian from his mouth as she touched and stroked everything. She kneaded his buttocks shamelessly, traced his flank with questing fingers, touched and stroked every inch of tightly honed muscle.

And with each innocent touch of hers, he turned harder, and tighter, his rock-hard erection swelling in the groove of her thighs. The hard, velvet length, the sheer size of him made her mouth dry.

Her heart picked up pace as he kissed the rim of her ear and whispered, "Spread your legs for me, Pia."

Head bowed into his chest, Pia did. A jolt of sensation spread outward when he rubbed his shaft along her sex. Her breathing hitched to a faster rhythm and soon Raphael's joined hers. His one hand clasped both of hers above her head while with his other hand, he rubbed himself in her wetness.

"You're so perfect for me, Pia." Another slide, another shiver. Another sigh from her mouth. "As if you were made for me."

Slow shivers built in her spine at the slick slide of him against her. Even oversensitized from her climax, a whisper of sensation pooled again at her sex. And then, suddenly, he was inside her in a hard yet somehow smooth, unsuspecting movement.

Her spine bucking, Pia gasped at the invasion. Nails digging into his shoulders, she tried to buck him off but he remained lodged inside her.

It was as if there was a hot poker inside her. His body incredibly rigid, his muscles tense, Raphael whispered words against her temple, her eyes, her nose. Fervent promises to make it better, feverish endearments as if he couldn't bear to hurt her. "Look at me, *cara mia*. I promise you the worst is done."

Pia opened her eyes, terrified of showing him what she was feeling. Of making him think she didn't want this, didn't want him. But such a warm smile dawned in his eyes that it drove away her misgivings. "You're the science teacher, *si*?"

Her sex spasmed as if to remind her and he sank in a little more. "I'm sorry, Raphael. I… I didn't mean to…"

"No sorries between us, Pia. Not when I've to hurt you a little more before I can give you pleasure."

Tiny beads of sweat gathered on his forehead. His skin was like damp velvet under her fingers. He looked as if he was hewn from some rough stone, so stark were the bones of his face. He was exercising immense control, Pia realized, and felt like a big coward. "I don't care how much it hurts, please move."

"Kiss me, *cara mia*. Like you mean it," he added with a taunt.

Unclenching her fists, Pia took his mouth in a soft kiss. Hands in his hair, she pulled him down, angling his mouth the way she wanted it. It was the first time he let her drive a kiss between them. Liking the way he growled under her touch, Pia slid her tongue inside his mouth in a silky sweep that made him groan deep in his throat.

She peppered his jaw with urgent kisses, licked his neck like a cat, and then dug her teeth into the groove of his shoulder. A timely epithet flew from his mouth even as his hip jerked, sending sensation spiraling down her spine.

And just like that, slowly, her body got used to his invasion inside of her. She softened and stretched around him, a slow pulse of pleasure spiraling out from there. When he moved within her in soft, slow strokes, it was as if there was a poem of pleasure being written inside her. As if she were being taken apart and remade again within Raphael's hands.

Trusting some unknown instincts, Pia wrapped her legs around his back and he groaned his pleasure.

She'd always wondered at the raw intimacy, at the lack of inhibition that had to go hand in hand with sex, had always cringed at revealing herself like that. Yet nothing in the world felt more natural than being beneath Raphael, than meeting his eyes and sharing the pregnant moment, nothing more perfect than the sweaty shift and slide of their bodies against each other with pleasure billowing in their wake.

His hands under her buttocks, he lifted her until every hard stroke rubbed against her clitoris. Soon, the pressure built again until Pia came in a cataclysm of pleasure.

And he watched her, every nuance in her face, as if he owned her. With an intensity that sent aftershocks through her pelvis.

"You feel like heaven, *tesoro*, and I have to move," he said in apology.

Pia touched her fingers to his forehead, and the lock of hair that was always falling down. "I'm yours, Raphael," she whispered, her heart overflowing.

Her name on his lips, her body held down tight, Raphael thrust faster and deeper inside her. She felt his spine lock. With a guttural cry that she'd forever remember, he spent himself inside her.

With his hands tight on her hips, his heavy weight pressing onto her, her body felt as if it was being thrown around by a storm. Her breathing matching his rough rhythm, Pia couldn't let go of him.

Morning light was beginning to seep in through the curtains, bathing their bodies in an orange glow. He was hard and heavy over her, but deliciously so. Hadn't she heard some of her colleagues whisper that men always pulled away after they were *done*? That they didn't like clingy women?

She very much wanted to cling to Raphael, to breathe in the musky scent they made together, to soak in the wonderful warmth of his body. But she didn't want him to think she was getting all gooey and sentimental over what they had done, even though it was exactly what she was feeling.

Her heart dipped as he moved away from her. She scrunched her eyes tight and felt his eyes on her back. The sheets slithered around her, and she heard his soft tread on the floor. A sharp ache—one that rivaled the one in her body—filled her heart.

Raphael wasn't given to tenderness or sweet words, she told herself.

She didn't know how long it was—it felt like an eternity—before she felt him tugging the duvet from her tight fingers.

"Raphael, what are you—"

"Shh, let me."

When his hand reached her thighs with a cold washcloth, Pia flushed. "Raphael you don't have to—"

"*Si*, I do." His gaze held hers, a wealth of words that he wouldn't say in it.

Looking away from him, heat crawling over her cheeks, Pia gave herself over. With a gentleness that brought tears to her eyes, he finished cleaning her up. And then he was back in the bed before she could arm herself against the onslaught of emotions crowding her.

A warm glow fanned out in the regions of her heart. She ran her fingertips over the back of his hand, absently stroking the veins. The scent of their intimacy was a warm blanket around them.

The sudden realization that she could spend eternity like this hit her like an electric charge to the heart. He didn't want eternity. God, he didn't even want a few months.

"Turn around and face me."

When she stiffened, he pressed until she was on her

back. The smallest movement made her aware of the soreness between her thighs.

With his hawk-like gaze, Raphael caught it. A furrow came on between his brows. "Do you still hurt?"

Pia blushed, and then shook her head. Then she saw the uncharacteristic hesitation in his eyes. From everything she'd learned about him, she knew Raphael didn't do intimacy.

He tipped his head and took her mouth in a soft, tender kiss that made her chest ache. She would never tire of his kisses or that look he got that said he wanted to kiss her. He pulled her closer to his naked body and tucked his arm neatly under her bare breasts. Pia stiffened and tried to pull the duvet up.

A tussle resulted. She huffed. He growled. They made a compromise and pulled the duvet up over his arm while his hand cupped her breast.

"I like having you in my bed like this, knowing that whatever everyone else sees, I know the real, passionate you, *exploding like a firework*." He said it softly as if to let her get used to it. "Only me, *cara mia*." A long sigh left her and Pia settled into his embrace.

"Raphael, we need to talk—"

"No, what you and I need is sleep. Hours and hours of it. We'll only wake up when you're not sore and I can be inside you again. Until then, sleep, *tesoro*."

And just like that, Pia fell asleep.

The loud peal of Raphael's cell phone startled Pia awake. It took her a few seconds to orient herself but the soreness between her legs brought back awareness of the previous night.

She felt Raphael's kiss against her shoulder, and then his groan as the phone started again. The sheet held tightly with her fingers, she turned around to face him. Sleep

mussed, he was even more gorgeous in the morning sunlight.

With a gentleness that stole her breath, he pressed his
thumb against her lower lip. "You are good?"

She nodded, unable to find words that could sum up the
glorious feeling in her chest. And then, because she knew
he couldn't ignore whoever it was indefinitely, and because
she didn't know when she'd get a chance again, she pressed
a kiss at the hollow of his throat and licked his skin.

He groaned, kissed her hard, and then picked up the
phone.

Within seconds, the gentle lover disappeared.

With two rapid-fire sentences he finished the call,
whipped out of the bed and padded, utterly naked, into
the bathroom.

Hearing the shower run, she quickly pulled his T-shirt
on and sneaked down the corridor into the other bedroom.
She'd barely finished her shower and pulled on another of
his shirts when he walked in, a scowl on his face.

His jet-black hair was wet and dripping. Undone shorts
hung low on his hips. Pia swallowed the jolt of lust that hit
her low in her pelvis.

Before she could blink, he picked her up in his arms
and dropped her on the bed in his own room. "I told you
we're going to sleep around the clock."

Pia laughed and pushed her wet hair out of her face. She
didn't know whether to be mad or glad about his possessiveness. "I just... I've never been in a relationship like this
before and with you everything's muddied." She smiled
when he joined her on the bed and sat up with her tucked
between his legs. "I didn't want to assume."

"This is not an affair, *si*? What it is, we'll figure out
later."

Turning in his arms, she kissed his mouth full on. It

was a good minute before she let him go and by then they were both breathing hard.

"Raphael, who was that on the phone?"

"My lawyer. He's heard from Allegra now that she's out of the clinic."

"Your ex is out? How is she?"

"Apparently, she worked through the entire program, is certified to be drug-free and has her addictions under control, no boyfriends in tow, and is desperate to see Alyssa."

Pia wanted to ask for more information, dying to know about the woman who had once worn his ring. She rubbed her finger, and then dropped it when she realized what she was doing. "I heard your mother say she was extremely beautiful."

She cringed the moment the words were out but Raphael barely seemed to note the wistful tone in her voice.

"She's extremely beautiful, the life of every party," he replied with a faraway gaze, "and every man she knew wanted to possess her. I had the biggest bank account among the fools who pursued her and so she chose me."

"You can't believe she chose you just for that," she said, shocked by the depth of his cynicism. "You're a very—" He arched his brow and she flushed. "You know your appeal, Raphael. Modesty doesn't suit you."

"It was my pocket and my power that attracted Allegra. Not that my looks didn't help. Actions speak louder than words however much she professed to love me. All her behavior, that I was too besotted to see then, proved how much she cared for the status of being Raphael Mastrantino's wife and not at all for me and our marriage."

"So you have no culpability at all for its failure?"

"Not everyone wants to shoulder blame when it's not theirs. Frank took advantage of you. It's not your fault."

"But you loved her, didn't you? When they think I can't hear them, or maybe because they want me to hear it, people dissect your marriage. They talk about how you pursued Allegra for three years. They call it the match of the decade."

Trust Pia to drill down to the matter.

There was never judgment in Pia's tone. He wrapped his arms around her and pulled her tighter against him. He knew himself and yet every time Pia delved deeper, he found something new.

Not always good things, but things he hadn't known.

Jaw tight, Raphael pored over her question.

Had he loved Allegra?

Not that he'd had eyes for anyone but his stunning ex. He had been thinking with something other than his head.

Drunk on his success with Vito Automobiles, puffed up with power, he'd decided she was the perfect candidate long before she had set her sights upon him. He had pulled his family from scandalous ruin and bankruptcy and all that had been missing was the perfect society wife to complete his ascent.

"No, I didn't love her. And in hindsight, I wreaked even more damage on her than her mother had done with her affairs and her neglect. I should have never married her. She needed someone softer, kinder and I…all I wanted from her was a trophy wife."

He laid his head back against the headboard. *Christo*, of all the times to realize his faults. He couldn't soften toward his ex now.

"Isn't it good for Alyssa that her mother's worked through the program?" came Pia's tentative voice.

He shrugged. "It doesn't matter. I forgave her when she had affairs behind my back. I forgave her when she lied to me about—"

A hard gleam entered his eyes. But Pia was beginning to see beneath that hardness. Beginning to understand that

Raphael felt things deeply. More than even he understood. That he was just good at burying it all.

She pressed her face into his chest, feeling an overwhelming tenderness for him. And waited.

"I found her high at the house once with Alyssa barely a month old. Gio and her mother, even mine, they all pled her case. They said that addiction is like a sickness, that she didn't know any better. But she's an adult who's responsible for her actions. I won't forgive that. She's not getting her hands on my daughter in this lifetime."

"That sounds so final," Pia said, before she could stop. "Are you protecting Alyssa? Or punishing Allegra? Is it even about Allegra, or is it about your father?"

He looked so furious then that Pia braced herself for a cutting reply. She'd gone too far. Worse, they both knew she'd unwittingly struck on the truth.

"Only you could look beneath my anger for a junkie ex, Pia."

Something in his tone tugged at her. She longed to wrap her arms around him and hold him. To tell him that caring for someone was not weakness. That he wasn't invincible, whatever the world led him to believe. "I just… I think you've never forgiven your father for what he did."

He looked away but didn't deny it. "He had been my hero for so long. And then suddenly, one day he was gone, without a word."

And he'd left Raphael alone with a burden that would crush most seventeen-year-old boys. A burden he'd used to fuel his own ambition. A burden that his mother had continued to put on him.

"Raphael—"

"It's all in the past, Pia."

He took her mouth in a hard kiss that sent little waves of pleasure through her body. When he pulled her beneath him, when he rocked into her with the utmost tenderness because he was worried she'd be sore, when he kissed her mouth with warm languorous strokes, she gave herself over to him.

He loved her slowly, gently this time, as if she were breakable in his rough hands. He told her in sweet Italian what she did to him. But as their climaxes hurled them into ecstasy, as he tucked her under his arm, an ache unlike any she'd ever known settled in her chest.

Raphael might think it was in the past, but the mark was still there.

The anger, the hurt, were both still there buried under a hard shell.

He would never let himself weaken, never care again.

Pia knew it as surely as she did that she felt something more than attraction for him. Something more than admiration. And the scariest part was that she didn't know how to stop it.

CHAPTER ELEVEN

PIA DIDN'T SEE Raphael for another two weeks.

He wanted her. But whether he'd have acted on it if he hadn't been shaken by Gio's sudden heart attack, if he hadn't been vulnerable, was a doubt that gnawed at her constantly.

She was more aware of her body now than she had ever been before—aware that anytime she thought of them in that huge bed, her sex became damp and her breasts tingled; aware that anytime she caught even a hint of that aqua-based cologne her skin prickled; aware that when she touched herself when she was showering or when she was finding sleep hard to come by, her body ached for a more purposeful, knowing touch. Ached for him.

He hadn't forgotten her, that was for sure.

Because for every day she hadn't seen him, he had sent her flowers, a diamond bracelet by an up-and-coming designer whose pieces had year-long waiting lists, so Gio had informed her. She was determined to return it, but then came a brand-new coffeemaker with endless capsule refills because she'd been complaining that Italian coffee was too strong for her. And then one day, the present that had her heart thumping against her rib cage arrived: a high-end set of carving tools and a particular type of wood that she'd told him she couldn't source anywhere in the world.

Her heart warmed at the thoughtfulness of his gifts,

highlighting the contrast from when it had only been a pretense.

She didn't want things with Raphael to be over. She wanted more of his kisses and his hot caresses, his warm smile that only she brought out, and just more time with him.

She wanted a relationship with him.

But after the second week of still no Raphael, mild resentment and a gnawing anxiety settled on her. Especially when his mother took it upon herself to visit Pia and slyly let it drop that Raphael was dealing with matters relating to Allegra, who had briefly visited Alyssa two days ago.

More than once, Pia caught a hint of suggestion from Portia as to how hard Raphael had worked to build Vito Automobiles to what it was today. And how much Gio himself owed Raphael.

All she cared about was that he'd been so close and hadn't dropped by to even say hello.

At least her application to a prestigious online university to get her master's degree in education had been accepted—a dream of hers for so long. No sooner had she received the email than he had sent her a brand-new laptop, a box of chocolates, a pair of her prescription glasses because she'd told him she kept losing her first pair and misplacing the spare.

When Pia had laughed for two minutes straight, Gio had been utterly puzzled.

So most afternoons, Pia settled down in the veranda with her laptop and lesson plans while her grandfather napped. Afraid of creating even the smallest ripple through Gio's precarious health, she had abandoned her plans for leaving Italy for now.

So it was fifteen days later that she found Raphael standing in the courtyard with a glass of white wine in his hand.

He cast a tall shadow in the afternoon sun, his broad shoulders tapering into a lean waist and muscular thighs, the very ones that had cradled her. There had been such power, such strength in him and yet he had been so gentle with her. That she knew his body with such intimate knowledge sent a strange thrum of power flowing through her veins.

Not that she had any illusion that he belonged to her.

She doubted Raphael would ever truly belong to any woman. And yet, seeing him stand there, Pia could only feel tenderness for him. As if somehow she could bring a new facet out of this hard man. As if she could give him something he didn't have or hadn't known before.

She sighed and trudged up the steep path. His hair, grown overlong, curled over the collar of his shirt. A pang beat through her chest as she noticed the dark shadows he sported under his eyes.

Wineglass raised to his mouth, he froze when he spotted her. That intense stare of his made her pulse flutter, that familiar feeling of excitement and anticipation singing through her veins.

His dark eyes swept over her with such lingering hunger that Pia instantly knew that he felt this thing between them just as strongly as she did.

Sweat had gathered over her forehead and her neck for she'd been walking for almost an hour. Her hair was a nest around her face. She wished she'd worn anything but another pair of old jeans and a collared T-shirt.

Then hated herself for thinking that.

"Hello, Pia."

Pia walked around him, the clamor of her heart far too much to stand being near him right then, and poured herself a glass of ice-cold water. Only after she took a fortifying sip did she lift her gaze and meet his.

"Hello, Raphael."

The table stood between them, yet nothing could dilute the awareness singing in the air between them, or his displeasure. His fingers gripped the wine flute so tightly that she was afraid he would break it and hurt himself.

"You didn't come to the phone when I asked for you."

She shrugged while her grandfather watched them as if he were at a tennis match. "I just…it wasn't a good time to talk on the phone," she said.

"All five times that I asked for you?" His tone rang with disbelief. His gaze lingered on her lips, searching, seeking.

There were a thousand questions in that simple sentence and Pia couldn't answer all of them in front of Gio, even if she had the answers.

"I've been busy. Studying. I enrolled in a wood carving class in the village. Also thank you so much for the new tools and the wood. And the laptop. And my new glasses. I appreciate all the gifts," she said lamely.

He carefully put his wineglass down and folded his hands behind him. "Do you?"

She hesitated at his combative expression. "Yes."

"Tell him about the man you met when you went out to the *trattoria* the other night," Gio urged. "You're seeing him again, aren't you?"

Like a hound scenting prey, Raphael walked past the table toward her. "Who is this man?"

Pia glared at Gio. Really, she didn't understand Gio sometimes. Of all the hundred things he could've mentioned to Raphael her non-date was what he told him? "Just a guy I met at the café."

"Is he a local? Does everyone at the café know you're Giovanni's granddaughter? Why didn't Emilio tell me?"

"So Emilio is spying for you?"

"Emilio keeps an eye on Gio and now on you too."

"I'm not answerable to you. You're going to let him

question me like that?" She appealed to Gio when he finally put the phone down.

"Raphael," her grandfather said in a mock warning.

While she had been taking her stand, he had moved closer. The familiar scent of him—musk and heat—had her knees trembling beneath her. Pia clutched the table when he reached out a hand and brushed her cheek.

His hand pushed at a lock of hair behind her ear, while with the other he cupped her hip and pulled her forward. Her pulse racing, her body turned traitor, dipping toward him as if he were her true north.

"Are you trying to make me jealous, *tesoro*?"

Staring into his eyes, Pia forgot the entire world. "You're the one who jumped to conclusions. And I would never do anything so low."

"You wouldn't?" He looked at her as if she were the answer to a lot of questions. A thumb traced her jawline, resting at the corner of her mouth. "You still haven't told me anything about him."

"Christ, Raphael. He's a waiter at the café in the village. He saw me with some tools, we started chatting and it turns out carpentry is his hobby. We started talking, found we had a lot in common and when he told me about the class, I enrolled in it. That's it. I made a friend. Sometimes, we hang out at the café. I didn't know I was supposed to send you a day-to-day summary of my movements. I didn't know I wasn't allowed to make friends. Am I so untrustworthy? Am I answerable to you?"

"No, *cara mia*. Not answerable, and not untrustworthy, but you're…"

"Naive and foolish?"

"Innocent." How she was beginning to hate that word! "I do not care who you make friends with as long as the only man you let hold you like this is me."

"Raphael, please, can we—"

She never finished the sentence because he pressed his mouth to hers in a soft buss and she was instantly lost. Every slumberous nerve ending leaped to life.

Oh, how could she want him so madly and be so mad at him at the same time?

His lips were so soft and yet hard, so familiar and yet there was something new in his every kiss. She could spend a lifetime in Raphael's arms just savoring the taste of him, learning what he liked, discovering what she needed. Twining her tongue with his, Pia poured her heart and soul into his kiss.

When he held her like that, when he looked at her with such tender desire in his eyes, desire and love didn't feel so different. What resonated in her body seemed to calm the clamoring in her soul. When Raphael was near, everything in her lined up.

"*Maledizione*, but I have missed kissing these soft lips," he whispered into her mouth, sending arrows of pleasure to scandalous places. "Tell me you missed me, *cara mia*. Tell me you lie awake like me in the middle of the night wishing for my body, like I did for yours."

Vining her hands around his neck, she sank into his hard body. Soft groans rumbled from their mouths as, thigh to thigh, their bodies fit perfectly against each other.

Pia had no idea how far she would have gone, if he hadn't pulled back. It took her a few minutes to realize through the sensual haze that Gio had spoken.

She burned with embarrassment. Yet her grandfather ignored her completely, as if the responsibility of it solely lay at Raphael's feet. "Gio, it's only—"

Engaged in some macho one-on-one with Raphael, her grandfather wouldn't even look at her. "Pia, I would like to speak to Raphael alone."

She'd never been dismissed like that ever in her life before. "Not if you're going to discuss me," she said, frustration bleeding through her words. "Nonno, I know you worry for me and I didn't make it easy by trusting Frank but I can take care of myself and this is really not anyone's business but—"

"That cheating man is not my concern, Pia. Knowing what is at stake, knowing my worries and my plans for you, what my godson does with you *is*. Raphael, this has gone on long enough. Will you do the right thing or shall I—"

"Calm down, Giovanni," Raphael said softly, a hint of steel in his tone. "The status of our relationship was hardly crucial when you were lying in the hospital bed."

"And now?" Gio taunted.

Raphael replied in that same cutting voice that sent chills up Pia's spine. "Leave it to me."

Pia stared from one man to the other, feeling as if she were standing on ground filled with land mines. A sudden grin transformed Gio again to that loving, but cantankerous old man. Dread pooled in Pia's belly. "So, you two will be married soon?"

Words came to her lips but Raphael's grip around her waist tightened.

"As soon as I can manage it, *si*," Raphael replied, and Pia went utterly still.

It was as if someone had pulled the rug from under her. As if someone had punched her in the stomach in the dark.

Contrary to what would be expected of an eighty-four-year-old man who had just had two heart attacks in one year, Gio laughed heartily. "This year, Raphael." His bushy eyebrows scanned Pia's face. "You'll be happy with him, *piccola*."

Whatever protest Pia was about to make died at the transformation in his face. How could she do anything to ruin the happiness in his face? "Nonno, I'd like to wait until you're better before we even talk about the plans."

Gio nodded magnanimously. "I remember how glorious

it feels to be young and in love, but remember what happened with Lucia and me." He pulled Pia into his arms, gave her a kiss on her cheek, his eyes glimmering with tears. "Lucia would approve of who I found to look after you.

"Too much *excitemente* for an old man, *si*? I will go rest now."

Who I found to look after you...

The words left a chill on Pia's skin. There was something so very wrong with it but she couldn't put her finger on it.

The moment Giovanni's silver head disappeared behind the doors of the house, she jerked away from Raphael.

Just when she was beginning to accept that she wanted a relationship with Raphael, the idea of marrying him, the idea of being his equal, his lover, his wife sent her into a swirl of panic.

"Pia, wait."

"No, Raphael. I need to—"

She tried to slip away, but he captured her wrist and tugged her closer. Her legs tangled with his, her chest rasping against his. The man had the most beautiful black eyes. And when they focused on her like that, she was afraid she would melt from within. That she wouldn't be able to refuse whatever he commanded of her in that arrogant tone.

"Let me explain, *cara mia*. You will—"

Chest rising and falling, Pia faced him. "Don't call me that."

His fingers crawled to her bare arm, the length of them wrapping around it. "I will call you whatever the hell I please."

There was a possessive intensity to his words that shivered over her skin. He wasn't mocking her now and something clearly had upset him too. Not that he would ever admit to it. "But I'm *not* yours to call whatever the hell you please," she countered softly, staring into his eyes.

They flared infinitesimally, and Pia felt a surge of satisfaction amidst the panic. Did he really think she had no spine? "I didn't protest in front of Gio because I didn't want to upset him. Because I tried to understand that he called your honor into question. Clearly there's something going on between you two."

Inscrutability again. What were Gio and Raphael planning that she wasn't supposed to know? She hoped it wasn't another protective measure. "I've never seen you so upset before."

She fisted and unfisted her hands. "I hate lies. I hate deception of any kind and it is my grandfather we're deceiving."

"It's only deception if it's not true."

She flinched and stopped her frantic pacing. But he wasn't joking. Dear God, he looked absolutely serious! "I've not agreed to marry you. And I don't remember you asking me. So of course it isn't true, and ergo it is deception."

"If the lack of a proper proposal upsets you...?"

A hysterical laugh fell from her mouth while he stared at her with an inscrutable expression. "Stop saying I'm upset. I'm not upset. I'm just stating for the record that we don't even have a relationship."

"No?" His fingers clasped her bare arm and her breath fell out of rhythm instantly. "So you go around sleeping with men for the fun of it?"

"There's nothing wrong with sleeping with a man for the fun of it. Sex should be fun and positive and tender and breath-stealing, shouldn't it?"

A wicked gleam danced in his eyes. "I am pleased to have left you with such good impressions, *bella*. I agree that sex should be fun and positive and should be had whenever one wants to." Heat arced between them, his fingers crawling into her nape. A sultry invitation glimmered in his eyes.

On a soft whimper, Pia closed her eyes. Images of their long, sweaty limbs tangled in gray sheets, the sinuous whispers of their skin sliding over each other, Raphael moving inside her like music—the sensations inundated her.

"But we're not discussing the sexual mores of twenty-first-century women, are we? We're discussing you, Pia. I know that what happened the other night is not a small thing for you."

"No. But one night's incredible sex is not the basis for marriage either. You could have told Nonno that we're just…we're just…"

"Whether now or in a few months' time, we have to face this question, Pia."

"Maybe so. But you said you didn't want a relationship with a woman, much less to marry one."

"You think I took you to bed, took your virginity, without being prepared for the consequences? Do you honestly think we could have a red-hot affair under Gio's nose, and then go our separate ways? Turn the clock back to become polite acquaintances who have already shared lovers' intimacies? Will you be perfectly all right when you see me with a new woman?"

"Yes." She called his bluff while her heart thudded. "I'll be fine. We should stop now. Before all those scenarios could become true. Before one of us gets hurt."

Jaw clenched tight, he stood in front of her. "Is that right, *bella mia*? You have zero interest if I take another woman to my bed? If I push inside of her wet heat like I did with you, if I send her into ecstasy with my body and my fingers like I did you? If I—"

Pia cupped her hand over his mouth, unable to hear anymore. "I don't know how one night of sex has transformed into this. We don't suit each other. I'm not beautiful or sophisticated or any of the things that your other… your usual women are.

"And you…"

"And I what, Pia? Tell me how I do not suit you."

"You don't believe in love."

"You thought you were in love with Frank."

"You'll never let me forget that mistake, will you? You think I'm a foolish idiot. Why would you even want me as a wife?"

"I do think you're naive. But it is what attracts me to you. You're unlike any woman I've ever known. You're honest and open. You don't care about external trappings. Just as you know you can trust me, I know I can trust you with myself and even with Alyssa. We burn when we come together and if you put love aside, you and I want the same things out of marriage."

"Like what?"

"Fidelity, respect and lots of babies."

"You truly want more children?"

"Yes. Especially if they'll be nearsighted and smart and beautiful like you are."

"I have to think about it. I need more time. I need…"

"Si?"

"I want to spend time with you."

"I'm more than happy to do that."

She blinked. "You are?"

"Si, Pia. Usually when a man is attracted to a woman, and he wants to do all sorts of deliciously wicked things to her, and is determined to persuade her to walk down the aisle to him, he wants to spend time with her. He wants to be the one who brings her favorite things, he wants to be the one who makes her cry out with pleasure, he wants to be the one who gives her babies…"

Pia threw herself at Raphael, glad that they were finally

on the same page. "Although I don't think we should sleep with each other again too soon."

He looked thunderous. "What kind of a condition is that?"

"I go into this dreamy state where I can't think logically when we make love. I…what I'm saying is…you have too much power in this relationship if we have sex."

A hard, harsh laugh fell from his mouth. "You think you don't have any?"

A vein pounded in his temple as she pulled him toward her. Joy blooming in her chest, she wrapped her arms around his waist, ran her hands over his muscled back and down. How she loved the way he felt in her hands. When she slipped her hands lower to his buttocks and tugged, his arousal grazed her belly. "Do you think I do?"

Jaw tight, heat scouring those sharp cheekbones, he raised a brow.

"See, I didn't even know I had it." When he'd have slammed her body into his to cradle his arousal, Pia pushed back at his shoulders. "No, let me touch you as I please."

"You're playing a dangerous game, *cara mia*. It's been two weeks and I know if I touch you, you'll be wet for me."

Pia blushed, the dampness between her thighs confirming his arrogant confidence. "Yes, well, we already agreed that you can melt me like an ice cream on a summer day with one look, *si*?" She ran her hands up his back and sank them under his collar.

She petted him as if he were her very own wild animal. He growled when she rubbed herself against him. On purpose. Heat blazed in his eyes.

She was playing a dangerous game, and yet she'd never felt more alive. "Stay still for me, won't you, Raphael?"

His explicit Italian—about what he'd like to do to her instead—sent heat pooling in her lower belly.

Sinking her fingers into his hair, Pia kissed the corner

of his mouth. The scratch of his stubble against her lips was heavenly as she peppered that arrogant jaw with soft kisses. "I don't even know what I like and don't like yet."

"Let me participate and I'll give you the different options, *bella*. You love experiments, don't you?"

Laughter bubbled up her throat even as she nibbled on his lips as if he were her favorite treat. He tasted of wine and masculinity and seduction and it went straight to her head. And her buckling knees.

When she traced that lower lip of his that drove her wild, he sucked the tip into his mouth and released it with a pop. A whimper escaped her mouth, her nipples suddenly sensitive against her bra. On the next breath, his fingers crawled into her hair, held her tight, and he took over the kiss. Hard and demanding, he plunged his tongue into her mouth. Rising to her toes, angling her mouth, Pia gave back as good as she got.

Their teeth banged. Their lips nipped and bit.

His thigh lodged between hers, hard muscle rubbing against the apex of her sex. Just where she desperately needed it. "*Dannazione*, Pia." His forehead leaned against hers, his warm breath feathering over her face. "Come to bed, *cara mia*. I will happily show you how much power you have over me. We could spend all day in bed and by nighttime, you would know whether you like me above you, or under you or behind you.

I will show you how to use that sweet, deceiving mouth to drive me to the edge. I will show you what I can do to you here—" he emphasized by rubbing at the spot that ached for his attention "—that will…"

A rush of wetness filling her sex, Pia drew a sharp breath. And stumbled away from Raphael. The man could seduce her just with words.

And like her, he was breathing hard. His pupils dilated, his nostrils flaring, as if he had just engaged in a physical fight. The front of his trousers was tented and when her gaze lingered there, his growl was feral.

Raphael undone—or at least close to—was the most glorious sight she'd ever seen.

Swallowing away the longing burning through every inch of her, she slowly wiped the moisture from her lips with the back of her hand. "I know you want to spend the day with Alyssa and I have to study. But I've been dying to see one of the cars you've restored," she added. Proving to herself that she could affect him just as much as he did her was a small victory. But having won the battle, she wasn't really interested in the war.

A vein pulsing in his jaw, he stared at her for so long that Pia wondered if she had pushed him too far. "Friday evening."

When he passed by her without touching her again, her heart sank.

"And Pia?"

"*Si*, Raphael?"

"You *will* be my wife, and I know how to exact retribution."

CHAPTER TWELVE

TORTURE BEGAN TO take on a new personal meaning for Raphael over the next month, thanks to his unofficial fiancée's unwillingness to let him give them both what they desperately needed.

If he had thought Pia biddable, she had proved he was utterly wrong. *Dio mio*, under the naive, smiling, ready-to-please demeanor was a core of steely stubbornness.

When she'd said she wanted to spend time with him, she'd meant it. And not in his ex-wife or mama and sisters kind of way, where what they wanted was for him to show them off in their designer gowns, the latest of Milan's haute couture fashion, at parties, and theaters. Where they could show off their connection with Raphael Mastrantino, CEO of Vito Automobiles, a man with powerful friends.

With them, it was always about the glitter he could add to their standing in society. It was the veneer of power that spread to them when they could claim a connection to him. It was what Raphael could provide and nothing else.

But with Pia, *Dio*, when she'd said she wanted to spend time with him, she'd meant she wanted time with him. Learning about him. The two of them *hanging out* with each other.

It had become Raphael's favorite phase in all of the English language.

She had insisted that he show her the vintage car he

was restoring currently. So Raphael had taken her to his house in Como one afternoon. What he'd expected was for her to ooh and aah over it, and then expect him to show her the sights of Como, the only village along the lake she hadn't seen.

Instead, driven by Emilio, Pia had arrived in the cutest overalls he had ever seen. Uncaring of the fact that her hands could get greasy or that her hair would be messed up—though Pia's hair was always messy and he loved it like that—she had crawled under the hood with him, asking him to explain what it was that he was currently doing.

Talking about the chassis and suspension while the scent of her curled in his muscles, her hot breath stroked his cheeks—he had never had a more diverting evening.

They had ended it with a glass of Chianti and mac 'n' cheese that Pia had cooked in his kitchen, having informed him that that was the extent of her culinary abilities.

Having never spoken to another soul at such length about his passion, Raphael had spent most of their dinner in quiet rumination and with a burning need to peel the overalls off her lithe body. To kiss and lick every inch of her silky curves.

Sharing even silence with Pia was wonderful.

They had ended the night, because she had a test early in the morning, with a soft kiss that had left him with blue balls. But also with a thread of quiet, incandescent joy he'd never known before.

Another time, she had invited him to sit through her class, and then made him model for her first face carved from wood, because as she had put it, he had classically handsome features with a bold nose and an arrogant chin that would lend itself to that particular type of wood.

He had sat still for almost an hour while the minx had worked with her hands, only to find her dissolving into giggles when he'd asked her to show him what she had so far.

"*Mi dispiace*, Raphael. I'm so bad at this, I've made you into a monster," she had sputtered amidst her laughter. "I'll ask Antonio to sit for me next time." Of course he had said no, to which she had responded by crawling to him on her knees, tracing those blunt-nailed, callused fingers over his nose, temple and then over his lips. She had then taken his mouth in such an erotic kiss, swirling tongue and biting teeth and all, that Raphael had been harder than the block of wood, and said, "I can't bear to ruin this gorgeous face, Raphael."

Since he was busy with work and Allegra's custody suit, and she was busy studying and carving and meeting the new friends she had made, all they could manage one week was two evenings spent together holed up in Gio's study, which he had been far too happy to give up.

While Raphael had spread out his paperwork on the vast mahogany desk, Pia had settled her textbooks around the sitting area. It was the most enjoyable quiet evening of his life. The sight of Pia with her glasses perched on her nose, studious concentration furrowing her brow, had driven him half-crazy.

The thought of spending the next fifty years in such close quarters with her was surprisingly exciting. He imagined looking up from his work to find her gaze on him with a slight smile, sitting in comfortable silence but with an ongoing sizzling awareness; the absolute knowledge that it wouldn't make a difference to Pia if his assets grew another billion or not, or if he lost most of it with some bad decisions like his father. The trust that she would never stop looking at him as if he were the most perfect man she had ever met—it filled him with the desire to wrap his arms around her and never let go.

Locking the door against any servants, uncaring that

he was dishonoring her under Gio's roof, he had crossed the room, knelt in front of her, pulled her hair from the tight braid she had forced it into and drunk greedily from her welcoming mouth.

He'd meant to keep his word. He'd meant to let her come to him, to give her the time she'd asked for. And yet, her responsive moans had had him spreading her legs wide, pulling up the long skirt she had worn that day, and then kissing his way up the silky skin of her thighs, all the way to the damp center of her sex.

He had tasted her desire for him while she had sunk her fingers into his hair, gasping and moaning, scandalized by his actions and yet thrusting against his ministrations until she was falling apart against his mouth while digging her teeth into his lower lip. The most potent masculine satisfaction had surged through him when she had collapsed into his arms, limbs trembling.

Cheeks pink, breath serrated, hair in wild disarray and her eyes, those wide, deep brown eyes glittering with an emotion he didn't want to give a name to. *Dio*, she'd been the wildest, the most beautiful thing he had ever seen.

Fingers sinking in his hair, she had guided his mouth down to hers for a quick press. "I didn't know I could feel so much pleasure that I could happily die from it."

"You're not dying until I have punished you for your no-sex rule," he'd said, sinking his teeth into the rough cushion of her palm.

"Poor Raphael, it has been, what? Three weeks?"

A soft flick at the center of her palm with his tongue. Like a spark plug when combusted, she immediately slithered in his lap. "Five weeks and four days, you minx."

She had crawled to her knees, stroked her palms up his chest, cheeks flaming pink and with the most mischievous grin said, "Raphael, can I...?"

He hardened into stone. Her hands on his thighs, yes, but the shy desire, her hesitation, got him every time.

"Can you what, *cara mia*?" If she had asked the world of him, he would have agreed.

Her face burrowed into his chest, her fingers drawing mesmerizing lines on the back of his neck. "I… I want to return the favor."

He swallowed the jolt of lust that shot through him. "What favor?"

"I want to do to you what you did to me just now," she had finally whispered at his ear. "I want to make you lose control too."

How he hadn't combusted right there, Raphael had no idea. Wedged against the taut curve of her buttock, his erection had twitched in his trousers at her innocent suggestion.

"Are you agreeing to marry me then?" he'd taunted instead.

He had no idea what she'd been about to say because his infernal cell phone had rung, disrupting the pregnant moment.

Somehow, what had begun as a convenient arrangement had morphed. It wasn't just the prize of finally owning Vito Automobiles that lured him anymore. It wasn't the convenience of returning all the favors Gio had bestowed on him by marrying Pia. It wasn't taking on the responsibility to protect her and Gio's wealth.

It was Pia herself.

He knew as surely as the beat of his heart, while he waited at the center in front of Teatro Alla Scala for her to arrive for her special opera night, that he wanted Pia in his life.

He wanted the woman who looked at him as if he were the world to her. And in return, he would give Pia everything she could ever want, everything that he was capable of giving.

* * *

Pia stepped out of the limo on a side street, an unnecessary indulgence Raphael insisted on, and walked the last few steps to the front of the historical opera house Teatro Alla Scala and gaped with her mouth open. She could have just as well caught the light rail, but of course he wouldn't listen.

Glad that she had worn her soft silk emerald-green dress that made Milan's humidity bearable, she looked around herself. Typical of the busy city's evening, Piazza della Scala was busy and noisy, mostly with tourists. Locals, she'd learned, had already escaped to the beach, especially as it was the weekend.

She had barely breathed in the architectural marvel all around her when the hairs on her nape stood up with that familiar prickle. Turning around, she spotted Raphael instantly among the elegantly dressed men and women in front of the famous opera house.

Tall and wide and impossibly gorgeous, he stood out. His shoulders looked broader than ever in the handmade suit, his looks even more breathtaking in the magnificent lights of the square.

Clad in a black suit with a white shirt underneath, hands loosely tucked into his trouser pockets, he was leaning against a pillar and watching her with a curious smile playing around his lips. As if knowing that she wanted to linger, he crooked a finger at her.

That playful arrogance, that wicked promise in his eyes sent a shiver down her spine. He looked good enough to be devoured. And he looked at her as if he was ready to devour her.

It had been a whole long, utterly miserable ten days since she had last seen him, ten days since he had sent her into spasms of unbearable pleasure with his mouth at her most private place. Just thinking of that scandalous moment, the pleasure that had filled her sent blood rushing to her ears.

And he knew. Even across the ten feet or so that separated them, she could see the gleam of that hunger in his eyes, sense the attraction arc between them.

Heart beating a thousand beats a minute, aware of more than one woman stumbling to a stop at the breathtaking sight of him, Pia reached him.

He is mine, a part of her cooed in joy.

Holding her at arm's length, he swept that possessive gaze over her arms and shoulders left bare by the thin straps of the dress. A much-needed breeze wafted by, revealing the thigh-length slit in her dress. She saw him swallow as a partial view of her toned leg flashed and she was fiercely glad for swimming all those hours and keeping herself fit.

And then his arm was around her, his mouth at her ear. "I do not like any other man getting such a good view of your legs, *cara mia*. They are only for my pleasure, to be wrapped around my hips while I move inside you." His hand rested possessively on her waist as if to warn off any approaching man. "I think I like you all covered up in your jeans and my shirts."

Luckily, Pia wasn't required to respond as the ushers were showing them to their seats on a balcony, which she was delighted to find was an individual room with a private coat closet across the hallway from the box.

While Raphael exchanged words with the usher, Pia took in the historical circle-style theater that she'd heard so much about. The energy of the place was incredible. Gorgeously decorated in gold and stunning red velvet, the *teatro* was everything she'd hoped it would be. Pushing up her glasses, she began to people watch, because the women and men were dressed in elegant designer outfits that would probably rival the costumes themselves.

When Raphael tapped on her shoulder and showed her to a seat, Pia smiled sheepishly. "I'm sure my enthusiasm must look very *provincial* to you. But Nonni described this very theater to me so many times and all the wonderful productions she had seen here before she left Italy that I can't believe I'm finally here.

It feels as if I have waited forever to see this. I think she wanted me to come here too." Tears filled her eyes, a sudden ache filling her to her very soul.

She knew Lucia had come here with Giovanni once. The special friend her Nonni had always mentioned with melancholy in her eyes could be no one else. And yet, soon after, they had had a big row, and Lucia had fled Italy while Gio, in a fit of anger, had engaged himself to a heiress.

Suddenly, that Raphael had brought her to the same theater, to the same opera, struck a chord of fear through her. She shivered, and instantly Raphael pulled her into his embrace.

Pia hid her face in his chest, embarrassed by her irrational fear. This was ridiculous. She and Raphael were different from Gio and Lucia.

For one thing, they were older and wiser. They understood each other much better. And yes, at every chance possible, Raphael stubbornly claimed that he didn't believe in love while she still did. But hadn't he shown her that he cared for her in a million ways over the last month and a half?

Weren't actions worth more than words?

Despite his cynicism because of his marriage to Allegra, despite his hardened exterior from having to raise his family from sudden calamity to prosperity, wasn't his desire to marry her based on loyalty and respect? Didn't it prove that somewhere in his heart Raphael did care for her?

The man who had so ruthlessly accused her of being

an impostor and a cheat the night of the ball, the man who had threatened to cut his ex-wife out of their child's life, Pia would have never expected him to consider marriage at all.

But it was he who had accepted the consequences of their night first. He who hadn't hesitated even for a moment over the step they would have to take for the future.

What she felt for Raphael—she was so scared of calling it love—was so much more complex than what she felt for Frank. Frank had only pandered to what she had so desperately needed at that time in her life whereas Raphael could be infuriating and arrogant but he would never lie to her.

He would never deceive Pia, would never make her feel as if he needed an added incentive to be with her, to somehow make up for her plainness and her shyness. For the glitter she lacked.

So what if he would never admit in so many words that he loved her? Wasn't what they had better, more real than some notion of love she had cooked up in her head?

His abrasive palms covered her bare arms and moved up and down. "Your skin is ice-cold, Pia. What is it?"

"Nothing. Thank you so much for this, Raphael."

"Never apologize for your enthusiasm for everything in life, *cara mia*. Haven't I convinced you yet that your pleasure, in all things, leads to mine?"

Pia blushed and cast a confused gaze at the empty seats in some of the private rooms for the opera was about to begin soon. "Antonio told me this particular production of *Rigoletto* had been sold out months ago." She sat down next to Raphael and adjusted her dress. "Do you think they're late?"

"I asked a friend of mine to buy as many tickets as he could on this level."

"But why?"

"Because I wanted you all to myself. And I wanted this night to be special for you." Pia gasped as only now she noticed a bucket of champagne on the table and a small velvet box in his palm.

Her heart thudded. Her mouth went dry as he opened the box and pulled out a magnificent princess-cut diamond with tiny emeralds around it, set in a simple white-gold setting.

"Pia Alessandra Vito, will you be my wife?"

"Oh." It was all the sound Pia could make, all the response her brain could come up with. Because just as she knew this theater, she knew of this ring too.

It was the ring with which Giovanni had proposed to Lucia. The ring that Lucia had sent back to Gio after their fight. Another tremor slid down her spine as she stared at it.

Something about this ring made fear bubble up in her.

"Pia?"

She jerked her head up, met his gaze and the desire she saw there fragmented her silly fears. "I'm sorry. I... Gio gave this to you?"

"Si."

"When?"

A shadow fell over that dark gaze. "Is that important?"

The impatience brewing in his carefully controlled tone told Pia how insensitive she was being. Heart thundering, she extended her left hand to his and smiled. "Yes, I will be your wife, Raphael."

With a victorious smile, he slid the ring onto her finger. Pulling her down to his lap and sinking her hands into his thick hair, Pia poured herself into his kiss. His mouth was warm and fluid over hers. They kissed softly, slowly, nibbling at each other, playing with their tongues, until passion was simmering in their very blood. With an arch of her back, restless with need, Pia wiggled in his lap. The length of his hard erection caressed her buttocks, sending a groan from her lips.

With a chuckle, Raphael pushed her off him and settled her in the next seat. Still in a haze, Pia gazed widely and he brushed a kiss over her temple. "If you wiggle anymore in my lap like that, *cara mia*, I will shame myself and then we'll have to leave before you see this grand production of *Rigoletto*. And then you'll not forgive me for spoiling your evening."

A hush fell over the theater and the red curtains were pulling aside when Pia murmured, "I think I would forgive you anything, Raphael. As long as you keep kissing me like that."

Raphael gently tapped on Pia's shoulder while the audience clapped thunderously at the end of an outstanding performance of *Rigoletto*. This particular story wasn't a great favorite of his but even he'd been moved by the top-notch performances and the intricately detailed sets.

Or maybe it was the woman he had shared the experience with. The woman who now belonged to him, body and soul. For a man who had vowed never to marry again, it was a bit of a shock to realize he very much wanted Pia's soul to belong to him too.

A savage sense of satisfaction pounded through his veins, made even hotter by the magnificent drama they had just seen. Not even the pride he had felt when he had made his first million, or when he had bought back the house his father had lost to creditors, could parallel his sense of possessiveness as he stared at the diamond glittering on Pia's finger.

She hadn't come to Teatro Alla Scala on his arm because it was the "in" thing to be enjoying high culture or to be seen in designer outfits, but to immerse herself in the drama played out on stage. She had tears in her eyes because she could see the majesty of the theater through her Nonni's eyes and relive it for her.

Pia had watched transfixed, every emotion portrayed on the stage reflected on her own face.

And watching her, understanding the depth with which she felt things, Raphael couldn't help but be moved. Couldn't help but feel a strange turmoil that he couldn't calm.

They emerged from the theater into the pulsing energy of the pedestrian square. Something feral throbbed in his veins and since he didn't want to scare Pia, he offered, "We're mere steps from the Duomo. Would you like to get a gelato to cool off? Or a coffee, which by the way I should remind you is an *espresso* in Italy and not the watered-down junk you call coffee?"

She turned to him and the candid emotion he saw in her eyes rooted him to the spot. "Not tonight, thank you. Nothing could top that performance."

As if it were an uncomfortable, unwanted weight, she twisted the ring on her finger. She had fiddled with it self-consciously during the performance too.

"Pia, if you do not like the ring, we will get you something else. I could not refuse Gio in that moment but I will absolutely understand if it does not please you. I want you to have whatever you want, *cara mia.*"

"No, of course I love the ring, Raphael. Nothing could make this night more glorious than it already has been."

"Then let's finish it with some of the calamari you like so much. With Gio visiting his sister today, I'm sure you've forgotten to eat." He let his gaze settle on the upper curves of her breasts.

It was the first time Pia had worn something so silky and revealing. And it was driving him crazy.

"Because I can't afford to lose any of the few curves I have?"

The vulnerability in her eyes snagged at him. "Because

you're now mine to protect. I wish I could show you how perfect you are to me."

"I think I'm beginning to believe it."

"Bene." He inclined his head, waiting for whatever was in her head to come to her lips with bated breath, for he knew only one thing made Pia so self-conscious.

Even white teeth digging into her lower lip, she adjusted her clutch, and then looked up again. That hint of hesitation in those eyes pierced him. And made him wild with desire, for he knew what it meant. "I just want to go home."

But he still waited. He wanted to hear those words from her mouth. He wanted her surrender. He wanted her to choose this, him. Again and again. He had a feeling that even a lifetime wouldn't be enough. "I will take you home then."

"No."

Covering the distance between them, she laced her fingers with his, pressed her body to his in a side hug that sent a shudder through him. If they lived a hundred years together, he would never get used to how freely she expressed her affection. How easily and naturally it came to her to show what she was feeling. That diamond sparkling brilliantly on her finger reminded him that the generosity of her spirit was his too now. His to guard from anything that could hurt her. Including himself.

A weight unlike any responsibility he had shouldered so far in his life.

She made a moue of her mouth, and then completely negated the saucy effect by pushing her glasses up on her nose.

He chuckled.

"I don't want to go back to the estate and I don't want a gelato."

"No? What are you interested in then, *bella?"*

A soft kiss on his cheek. Her breath fluttering over the rim of his ear. And then those warm brown eyes pinned him.

"You." There was no coyness in her gaze. No sultry invitation. No feminine arch of her body or fluttering of her eyelashes. Just pure, artless need. "Tonight, I want you, Raphael. Just you."

CHAPTER THIRTEEN

By the time she and Raphael rode the glass elevator to his ninth-floor apartment, Pia's nerves had stretched to breaking point. Desire was a live wire left unearthed between them as they sat at the ends of the seat in the taxi, speeding through the seven or so miles to his apartment in the affluent fashion district, a world away from the busy nightlife through Corso Venezia.

Raphael's cell phone gave that shrill ring the moment they stepped inside and Pia almost jumped out of her skin.

His hand at her lower back, Raphael steadied her. His own pithy curse when he looked at the screen painted the air blue. "I have to take this call."

While Pia stood there in the middle of the huge lounge, her pulse ringing like a bell all through her body, Raphael returned, after only a few minutes. His mouth took on that hard cast that she didn't like. Another darker tone added to the awareness sizzling between them.

She thought they'd grown comfortable with each other over the past few weeks, that they had crossed a milestone in their relationship, had gotten closer emotionally too.

Yet it seemed that all it took was one of them to give voice to this need between them, to express desire for sexual intimacy—she blushed when she realized that was what she had done—and every word became explosive, every look rife with promise.

"Who was that?"

He shrugged off his suit jacket, carefully folded it and left it on the chair. "Nothing important."

Struggling to keep her dismay off her face, she said softly, "That's what you say when you don't want to tell me."

His fingers stilled on his shirt buttons. "I don't want to tell you because it's not important."

"And yet, it made you curse like that? I've seen very little that causes you to lose your arrogant confidence. I know you're used to keeping matters close to your chest, that you probably never had a chance to confide in any—"

"It does not concern you, Pia. *Bene?*"

A sudden prickling heat behind her eyes, Pia simply nodded.

Raphael exhaled harshly, the tight line of his shoulders relenting. His hair, already messed up by Milan's humidity, became a little wilder when he pushed his hand through it. "I did not mean to be short with you." A sigh that made that broad chest rise and fall. "*Mi dispiace*, Pia."

Whatever hurt she had felt, his genuine apology instantly placated it. The matter was nowhere near resolved, she knew. It was her right as his future wife, it was her deepest wish that he share everything with her. But Pia had enough patience to wait. In every way, Raphael had proved that he was worth waiting for. "It's okay, Raphael."

"You mean it, don't you?"

"*Si.*"

His dark eyes, liquid with desire, swept over her. "I knew there was more than one reason I wanted to marry you."

Swallowing away her own anxiety about what was coming, she wanted to do something bold but in the strange mood he was in, it was hard to hold on to her newly discovered confidence.

"Would you like something to drink? I have some nice Chianti."

Despite the thick tension in the air, Pia smiled. She loved that he always remembered those small details. From the most trivial to the most important, he was always looking out for her. Part of it, she knew, was his nature. That sense of responsibility that had fallen on his shoulders at a young age had never quite left him.

He was one of those alpha males who walked into a situation and immediately took charge of it. Protected the innocents and chased away the threats. And remained aloof even amidst a crowd.

Part of his protective instincts toward her were also because she was Gio's granddaughter. And he was big on loyalty.

But a small part of it, she hoped, was because of what she meant to him. Was because of who she was.

She covered the few steps between them, until the tips of her breasts were barely grazing his chest. "I feel like I'm already drunk. So no thank you."

He grabbed her wrists and pushed them behind her until the front of her was pressed deliciously up against his hard body. "Always so polite." His mouth flicked a silky, wet trail from her jaw down to the crook of her neck. He sucked her skin rough and hard. Pia jerked as wetness rushed between her thighs. She couldn't even clench them because he had jammed his hard thigh between hers. "Raphael, wait…"

"Always so ready to forgive and forget. Always so generous."

A keening moan rose from her throat as his wicked tongue softly licked the hurt he had inflicted with his teeth. Pain and pleasure fused, love and desire roped together and ran hot like a cocktail through her blood.

Somehow she managed to pull back, clasped his jaw

and forced him to meet her gaze. "Raphael, will you not tell me what has made your mouth become hard again?"

His hands started torturing her then, stroking up and down her back, kneading her hips, cupping her behind until his arousal pressed against her lower belly. Her temperature shot up ten degrees at the least. "My mouth becomes hard?"

"Yes." She moaned when he rubbed it against her. "And you get that look in your eyes." With a half sob, half smile, she caught his hands with hers. "You have just asked me to be your wife and I accepted. You cannot hide things from me now. I want to share everything, Raphael, the good and the bad, with you.

I want to be here when you need me, just as you were there for me when I needed you."

She had no idea if she had gotten across to him. But when he raised his head and looked down at her, there was a dark glitter in his eyes. "There is something I need from you tonight. Will you give it to me?"

"*Si*. Anything."

"Undo my cuffs."

Taking his left wrist in her hands she undid the cuff links. And then repeated the same with the other hand. He unbuttoned his shirt and threw it off those broad shoulders. The sight of his lean chest with all his skin stretched taut over it made Pia tremble.

"Take off your clothes for me."

Instantly, Pia froze. "Here?"

"Here. Now."

"You did say anything," the devil said, taunting her.

She tilted her head. *"Bene."*

If this was what he wanted, then he would get it. She held his gaze, letting the slumbering heat in it drive her. She trusted Raphael with everything she had in her, so her shyness, her insecurity about her body, was nothing but a small barrier to cross.

She moved her hand to the zipper hiding on the side of her dress and pulled it down. The quiet rasp of it was loud in the silence.

Her movements were clumsy when she pulled the straps down. Dark eyes watched her the whole time and flared when the silky material fell to her hips and her breasts were bared. Pia shivered, less from the breeze that flew over her heated skin and more from the dark hunger in his eyes.

Her breasts felt heavier, the nipples turning into aching points as his gaze lingered there with barely hidden fascination.

"Push it down all the way. And step out of it."

Pia did as he bid, the last of her shyness leaving her at his quicksilver reaction. He was right. She had just as much power as he did in this situation. Her dress whispered to the floor, and still in her heels, she kicked it away.

She lifted her chin, daring him to go on, even as a thousand butterflies danced in her belly. His gaze moved from her breasts to her midriff and then lower. The flimsy white underwear she wore did nothing to hide her from him.

"Are you wet for me?"

Heat burst inside of her like a hot geyser, spreading to every nerve ending. "Raphael, *per favore*…"

"I wish to know, *bella*."

"I'm ready for you. I was ready for you when I saw you leaning against that pillar. When the Duke mercilessly seduced Gilda. When Rigoletto hired that assassin. When Gilda sacrificed herself for her unscrupulous lover. There, are you satisfied? Can you please take me to bed now?"

"Not yet." A silky smile curved his mouth. It seemed he was bent on pushing her to the edge now. "Come here and undress me."

She blinked.

He raised his brows. "I would like to be naked now, Pia."

She would not admit defeat tonight.

She walked toward him, stopped when the scent of him coiled through her veins. His trousers did nothing to hide his need for her. Swallowing, she set her fingers to work undoing his fly and then sliding them under the elastic band of his boxers pushing both of them down.

The turgid length of his erection sprang free, the soft head flicking her palm. Her sex clenched, and a gasp emanated from the depths of her.

It was all she could do to pull her gaze away from it and lift it to his face. He stepped out of his trousers and flicked them to the side with his feet, bold and utterly masculine. "Remember what you offered that night in the study? Is it still on, Pia?"

Just the thought of it made her skin tighten over her muscles. "Yes, the offer is still on."

Holding his dark eyes, she sank to her knees. His erection lengthened even before she touched it, sending a surge of power through her. Whatever it was that he thought she was not equal to, she would prove him wrong.

She was more than enough woman for Raphael Mastrantino.

"I want to make every fantasy of yours come true, Raphael. So you have to tell me if I do this right or wrong, *si*?"

Raphael's heart pounded in his chest as Pia obediently sank to her knees. *Dio mio*, he'd been angry at Allegra's latest trick to get custody of Alyssa.

After all her affairs, to claim that he was not a suitable father… His mood had instantly darkened. And when Pia so innocently offered to share his worries, he had worked himself to a dangerous edge.

He had only issued his command as a dare. As a way for

him to fight the all-encompassing emotion he was beginning to recognize in her gaze. To bring this thing between them back into his control. Because, sometime between beginning the evening with Gio's ring in his pocket and ending it with Pia telling him that she wanted *just him*, something had changed.

Even with Allegra's ridiculous claim, he still had everything he had ever wanted. So where was this dread in his heart coming from?

Any further thought on the matter shredded into nothingness when Pia took him in her hands and closed her calloused fingers around his shaft. His breath left him in a sibilant hiss when she stroked his rigid length in slow, cautious, almost-feathery movements.

Hair like a golden cloud around her face, the line of her spine a sensuous path, she had never looked more beautiful.

His nerve endings fired at her inexperienced, innocent touch, more than with any practiced lover's caress.

He looked down, hoping that the wide-eyed innocence of her face would smash his dark mood. But instead he found her opening that pink mouth wide and dipping it toward his erection.

His heart thumped against his rib cage.

Her small breasts with their pink-tipped nipples. Her toned thighs tensing at her stance.

It was an image that made him far readier than he wanted to be, after a month of deprivation.

At the first slide of the welcoming wet warmth of her mouth over his length, his hips thrust forward. A thrill ran up the back of his thighs pooling in his groin. He cursed hard and long, sweat beading along his skin.

The sound of her soft sucks sizzled amidst his harsh breaths.

Dio mio, had she any idea how she was destroying him?

A soft gasp fell from her mouth as he thickened a little more. Fingers delicately wrapped at the base of the shaft, she looked up at him, liquid desire making her eyes look like warm inviting pools.

"Am I pleasing you, Raphael?" *Christo*, even her question was artless. She did really want to please him. Not as a challenge, not for a dare. Not to prove to herself or to him that she had power over him.

But for the simple reason that his pleasure mattered to her. This intimacy between them meant something to her.

More turned on than he had ever been in his life, he sank his hands into her hair and guided her mouth the way he wanted it. Told her how much pressure he wanted and where he wanted it. Told her to use the slide of her silky tongue against his length.

As if she was one of her dedicated pupils that she often talked about, Pia followed his instructions to the letter. Soon, he was reaching the edge and the last thing he wanted to do was terrify her by pushing this into something else. He knew what it had taken her to accept his challenge. What she'd had to overcome because she wanted to please him more.

And that blunted the edge of his desire more than anything else. Wrapping his fingers around her wrists, he pulled her up roughly, lifted her in his arms and carried her over to the bed.

Warm skin, and trembling muscles, she was a lush invitation. And his for always. Every night and every day, she would belong to him. And he would touch no other ever again.

The realization made the moment even more poignant, raised it from just sex to something else.

She moaned as he joined her on the bed and covered her body with his. Protested with her nails on his back when he took her mouth in a leisurely kiss. Bucked up when he skimmed his mouth over her taut nipples without taking them into his mouth.

Her soft mewls goaded him on and on.

Flipping her pliable body easily, he separated her legs until she was straddling his arousal. Her spine arced under his touch as the softest, hottest part of her pressed against his erection.

She was damp and ready for him.

"I need you, Raphael, now," she breathed, writhing her body over his. With her eyes closed, her unruly hair flying around her face, her high breasts beckoning him, she was a potent invitation.

Slowly, softly, he brought her down on him so she could feel every last inch of him. He spread the lips of her sex with his fingers, the sight of her taking him in incredibly erotic.

Her low moan made him lose the last bit of control. He wanted her far too much and found himself thrusting, hard and rough, up into her snug sheath until he filled her completely.

Her shocked gasp rent the air.

"Pia? *Cara mia*, did I hurt you?"

Spine still arched sensuously, she bent toward him until the peaks of her breasts rubbed against his chest. Her eyes were glazed, a soft smile spreading her mouth. "*No.* I just forgot how it feels when you're inside me. And this way…" She flexed her hips in an age-old feminine rhythm and he sank deeper with a muttered oath. "This way…you feel like you're everywhere."

She took his hand and brought his palm to her heart, where it thudded. Her skin was damp to his touch, the scent of her arousal coating the very air he breathed.

Her eyes, crystal clear in the soft light of the evening, pinned him. "You're here, Raphael, in my heart too. Did you know? Somehow, you have made me fall so utterly in love with you."

Everything froze inside Raphael as his brain struggled to process those heartfelt words. Words he thought he was ready to hear, words he had even thought his due because that was the only way Pia would enter a marriage. Words he hadn't realized would steal the breath from him, would knock him out at his knees.

Mere words had never meant anything to him before, so how could it feel like hers could pierce him clean to his soul?

With a glorious smile, Pia pulled herself up and ground down on him. Sending pleasure pulsing through his groin. Her declaration rang in his ears as his body drove deeper, faster, again and again into her slick wetness.

Her moans surrounded him as he pulled himself up and stroked her swollen clit with every thrust. Something let loose within him, and he wanted to wring every ounce of pleasure from her body.

He wanted to give her this, because it was the only thing he had to give.

Soon, she was exploding around him, her muscles clenching him and releasing him in a cataclysm of pleasure. It spurred him on to his own mind-blowing climax.

But still she was not done. While his lungs struggled to draw air, she bent over and pressed a damp kiss to his mouth. The scent of her and him and sex was a potent cocktail in the air, a heady drug that he wanted every night.

"*Ti amo*, Raphael," she whispered, with a shy smile. Before Raphael could even wrap his mind around her words, around the truth of it shining in her eyes, she fell asleep on his chest, with him still lodged deep inside her.

Raphael woke up when dawn began to paint pink fingers over the sky. With a warm, silky-soft body tucked up into him as if it was made for him. As if she was the part that completed the puzzle that he hadn't even known was incomplete.

Sinking his free hand into her thick hair, he gently pushed it back from her face. Long lashes drew crescent shadows under her eyes, which sported dark circles. Had she been studying for some infernal test again? Had he tired her that much with his relentless need for her?

It seemed as if her words had unlocked some fathomless desire in him, for the more he had her, the more he wanted her.

Even in sleep, her face lost none of its artless charm. Something snagged in his chest as she burrowed deeper into his arms. *Maledizione*, but her trust in him was absolute, limitless.

Having never been on the receiving end of such unconditional, nonjudgmental emotion, he didn't know how to handle it. A part of him wanted to distance himself from her, wanted to slam the door on whatever she had opened between them.

He wanted to wake her up and say, *Demand something from me. Ask for something in return.*

If she didn't, he felt as if he would never know the value of what she was giving him. As if he would never recover his balance in this relationship.

She wriggled again with a soft huff, and his body came alive.

His arm was tucked under her breasts, her head in the groove of his arm. The lush curves of her buttocks pressed against his groin invitingly and his erection twitched and lengthened in greedy response.

He let his gaze linger over her naked body. And felt a jolt of shame when he saw the imprints of his fingers over her hips and inner thighs. *Dio*, he was a civilized man, not an animal. And yet, the thought seemed to have no control over his libido.

Careful not to wake her, he pulled his arms from under her and slipped out of the bed.

After a quick shower where the innocent enchantress had once again sent his lust into overdrive, where he had quite mercilessly pounded into her already-used body, he had barely toweled her dry before she had fallen into a deep sleep.

But even as those long lashes had been fluttering closed over luminous eyes—how had he never realized how big her eyes truly were behind those spectacles?—and her breath had been slowing down, she had kissed him softly. Slowly, as if in his mouth lay the key to her dreams.

Her cheeks had been pink, her eyes shining with that love she so easily whispered about to him.

Just you.

No two words had ever caused such a powerful longing to rush through his body. Struck such deep fear into him.

He hadn't been *just Raphael* in a long time, if ever.

He had been a scholarship engineering student at university, a son who had lost his father amidst a financial scandal and not allowed time to grieve, a young man who had suddenly become responsible for the pampered lifestyles of his mother and sisters, a man driven by ambition to wipe clean the scandal associated with his father's death, a protégé under the genius of Giovanni Vito, and then finally a CEO who had chosen and pursued the most beautiful, the most glittering, insubstantial butterfly of a woman to be his trophy wife.

But the way Pia looked at him, with startling emotion from the depths of her warm brown eyes, for the first time since he had accepted Giovanni's unspoken challenge, unease settled in his chest.

If all the trappings of his wealth and status were removed, if his ambition and his driving need not to become his father or share his fate were removed, then who was he at his core? Without the shame he felt for his father's failure, the bitterness brewed for years by his mother's careless callousness, the cynicism he had developed in order to bear Allegra's affairs—who was he then?

Had Gio ever wondered if that man was good enough for his precious Pia Alessandra Vito?

CHAPTER FOURTEEN

NOTHING, IT SEEMED to Pia, had gone right the day of her engagement party to Raphael.

The mid-October day had dawned sunny enough, with just the right amount of chill in the air. Pia's usual breakfast with Gio on the small veranda, the perfect start to her day, hadn't happened because he'd been interrupted yet again by a call from one of his sisters and he'd left immediately.

Pia had begun to dislike Thea Rosa quite a bit, for she seemed to delight in torturing Giovanni with all kinds of escapades at her old age.

So she'd breakfasted alone. All her misgivings about Raphael had grown into an insurmountable obstacle.

The toast she'd had sat in her tummy like a piece of lead, hard and unforgiving. And since she hadn't been paying attention, she had accidentally spilled hot water over her fingers and scalded herself.

What, or rather who, she really wanted was Raphael. They hadn't seen each other for a fortnight and Pia felt quite a juvenile resentment that his business always seemed to take him away when she needed him the most.

Just as he'd been unavailable the day she'd realized her period was three weeks late and had freaked out. After the first night with Raphael, she'd immediately gone on the pill. He was the one she wanted to freak out and panic with, since he partly shared the blame if she were pregnant. But no, Raphael had been in blasted Tokyo negotiating a new trade agreement between Vito Automobiles and a Japanese manufacturing company.

Instead, she'd had to beg Emilio to drive her to a pharmacy at least twenty kilometers from Gio's estate and Como where Raphael lived, to buy a pregnancy test. And then she'd performed the test in secret, because she was terrified of a servant finding out and telling Gio before she'd had a chance to process it and told Raphael.

Fortunately, the test had been negative.

Yet Pia had sat in the restroom for half an hour, feeling an inexplicable but violent urge to cry.

What she'd wanted then was the solid, comforting presence of the man she loved. The man who it seemed took care of every small thing for her.

On his return from Japan, Pia had broached the subject of his cutting down at work, and had received the most piercing stare leveled at her. He hadn't shut her down as he usually did but he hadn't responded to her suggestion either. Even Gio had backed her, saying he could delegate more.

"My father delegated, he trusted people he shouldn't have and his business sank within two years," had been his reply.

Since she didn't want to hurt him, and his father had always been a touchy subject with Raphael, Pia had left it at that.

She had let a lot of things slide, she realized now, but weren't those the growing pains of a new relationship? Pia had learned that Raphael, even after being married once, rarely, if ever, shared his thoughts with anybody. He was used to going it alone, used to that role of problem solver so much.

But the more they saw of each other and the more they had planned their engagement, the more Raphael had begun retreating from her. He'd become the stranger she had met that first night, brooding and unapproachable, except for the fact that she was allowed to sleep with him now.

Like clockwork, he either brought her to his apartment, kept her up until dawn—not that Pia wasn't just as voracious for his touch, for his possession—or he came to her at Gio's house, long after Gio and the staff had gone to bed. Usually, he found Pia studying or working on her toys.

When she was, he shed his shirt and shoes and waited for her to finish—as if she could make sense of a single line when his mere presence fried her brain. And then he took her to bed.

And every time, he made love to her—whether tenderly or with a fierce passion that left her sore for hours later—Pia couldn't stop the words of love tumbling from her mouth. Because it was only there she found the Raphael she had fallen in love with. Only there that he opened up to her. Only there was he not a stranger.

Three weeks later now, her period had started, and then stalled after a day. Pia had no choice except to ask one of Raphael's sisters to recommend a gynecologist and claim a ghastly yeast infection to silence the instant speculation written on all four of his sisters' faces as well as on Portia Mastrantino's.

Raphael was out of town. He wasn't flying in until a couple of hours before their engagement party. And again, Pia found herself battling the most inexplicable urge to cry.

No, not inexplicable anymore, if she were honest with herself.

Something had changed, she now realized since the night at the opera. Since Raphael had received that phone call? Since she'd agreed to marry him?

No, since she had told him that she had fallen in love with him.

It clicked like the missing piece of a puzzle that had been tying her up in knots.

That was it, the moment when everything had changed. The moment Raphael had begun withdrawing from her.

Why? She hadn't demanded anything of him. She had never said it with an expectation that he would reciprocate. She had only said it because she loved him. God, she loved him with everything in her and she wanted him to know it. She wanted him to know that she appreciated him, that she understood why he would probably never say it back. That she loved him just as he was.

Had he lost interest in her because of that? Had her appeal dimmed as a result?

She had heard talk among his mother and sisters that Allegra was back in Milan. That he'd been seen with her at a new restaurant. For a split second, Pia's faith in him had wavered. Even when she prodded, he barely said two sentences to her about Allegra.

Did he want to be back with his ex? Had she paled in comparison to the famed beauty?

No, something in her whispered.

Raphael was not some fickle boy she had a crush on. Raphael would never break her trust in that way. He thought her naïveté, her lack of sophistication was attractive. That it made her unique.

Yet, all afternoon, the question of his withdrawal gnawed at her soul.

Her fingers burning, her stomach in a constant knot, Pia watched in dismay as a small battalion of workers arrived in the huge open area in front of the house and began putting up a snow-white marquee of humongous proportions.

Fifteen minutes later a party organizer, an army of catering vans and then another crew of workers to decorate the tables arrived.

She hurriedly called to Portia, who had put the party

together, that there must be some mistake. Only to be informed that there wasn't. Two hundred and fifty guests were arriving to celebrate Raphael Mastrantino's engagement to Giovanni Vito's granddaughter.

The board of Vito Automobiles and all of their families, major shareholders, Gio's extended family, all of the million Mastrantino cousins and their families—it seemed the entire world wanted to see Raphael and his new fiancée.

"They all want to make their nods to Raphael. I mean, they always knew this would happen, but now it is more... definite, *si*?" Portia had said over the phone.

When Pia had whispered that she didn't actually understand, Portia said "When Gio declared you his granddaughter and his heir, it created problems for my Raphael."

"But why?"

"Because Giovanni and Raphael both own thirty-five percent each of VA's stock. With your appearance, it became clear that whoever married you would inherit that stock. So there were some who thought Raphael would not remain CEO for long. My son is a ruthless businessman and not everyone likes his principles, his practices. Some thought they would betray him and make good with the man Gio chose for you." Knuckles white, Pia gripped the phone, nausea rising through her throat. "But now that Raphael is marrying you, everyone wants to cook favor with him again."

The phone dropped from Pia's hand and clattered to the ground while she grappled with the truth.

Pia heard Portia's stilted English still coming from the phone, saw the decorators pull out rare orchids in droves, and it was all a haze as she walked back to her bedroom.

Now that Raphael was marrying Pia, there would be no contest for the CEO position. With 70 percent of the controlling stock in his hands, no one would ever again rival Raphael's powerful position. No one would ever take away the most valuable thing from Raphael—his wealth, his status and more than anything, his power.

For that was the only thing that defined Raphael Mastrantino.

And that power was the only reason he had proposed to Pia.

Because, she knew without doubt, Giovanni would have given Raphael Vito Automobiles for only one thing in return.

A ring on her finger.

With Gio nowhere to be seen, and family members—both Vitos and Mastrantinos—arriving as early as four, Pia found no respite anywhere in the house. Not that she could escape the misery of her own thoughts if she were alone.

At the risk of seeming churlish to Portia and Raphael's sisters, she had refused to dress for the party. At least not until she saw him. Not until she cleared up this matter with him.

Dressed in jeans and a sweatshirt of Raphael's that she had borrowed from his apartment one night, she was about to bolt to a café in the village when someone grabbed her and pushed her into Gio's study, thankfully empty of well-meaning relatives.

Raphael stood leaning against the door, devouring her as hungrily as she did him.

The sight of him hit her hard, sending such a pulse of longing through her that she swayed. His clothes for once weren't perfect, his eyes sported dark circles.

And yet he was so dear to her heart. An extension of herself.

Other things were more important to him than her. Even that she had accepted. But if the very foundation, the existence of their relationship was because she was Gio's heir—could she live with that?

"Ciao, bella."

"Did you just get back from Tokyo?"

"Not ten minutes ago."

"Raphael, we have to—"

Not a word emerged from her mouth before he slammed her into the door none too gently and his mouth covered hers. All her misery evaporated under the hungry on-slaught of his lips.

"Dio, I have missed you, I have missed this body and now the bloody house is crawling with cousins and aunts." His lips fused to hers, his hand crawled under the sweat-shirt that she was wearing.

Filling his hands with her breasts, he growled his ap-proval at her braless state. Past the point of no return, even knowing that this passion would only make things worse when she confronted him, Pia couldn't stop him. Couldn't stop herself from mindlessly rubbing up against him. Couldn't stop herself from stealing this incredible pleasure, this closeness with him.

"I missed you too." She pulled at his hair and bit his lower lip, frustration making her reckless. "I needed you, Raphael, God, how I needed you." A strangled cry escaped her when he rubbed his whiskers against her nipple, and then ensconced it in the wet warmth of his mouth. "I hate your job. I hate that you're never there when I need you. I hate that—"

His teeth tugged gently at her nipple and Pia lost ra-tional thought.

As if sensing her own edgy need for him, a torrent of Italian fell from his mouth. He praised her, he told her in elaborate detail how much he had missed her, how he had taken himself in hand one night in his hotel room imagin-ing it was her mouth again. Pia was sobbing by the time he unzipped her jeans and then his trousers, begging shamelessly for him to do all the things he was promising by the time he lifted her up against the door.

She wrapped her legs around his hips and he drove into her wet heat.

Guttural groans colored the air.

Head thrown back, arms vined around his neck, Pia gave herself over to the incredible sensation spiraling through her pelvis as Raphael plunged and withdrew with sure, fast thrusts.

And lost in the indescribable pleasure, lost to the magic he wove, she couldn't stop the words. "I love you, Raphael…and I hate you for what you're doing to me."

His sweat slicked body stilled around her, his dark eyes staring at her with shock. Tense muscles jutted out of his shoulders.

"Pia?"

But far too gone now, Pia buried her mouth in his neck and bit him, urging him to move.

On the next thrust up, he kissed her. Tongues tangled, teeth bit. And he moved inside her, with desperately hard thrusts, without the finesse she had come to know from him.

They exploded together within seconds of each other, their harsh breaths a symphony in the silence.

With her body's utterly explosive climax came Pia's tears, releasing everything she had been holding on to so tightly for weeks, afraid that if she voiced it, it would all fall apart.

She pushed at his shoulders and Raphael pulled out of her and slid her down to the ground gently. If he hadn't held on to her, Pia would have slithered into a heap on the floor.

The scent of him curled around her. Made her body and mind automatically think he was hers. That he would never deceive her.

God, she was a naive idiot.

With gentle movements, he straightened her clothes. Pia jerked away from his touch. A guilty flush scoured his cheeks as he took in her actions. His mouth tightened, deep grooves etched around it.

"Please, let me go."

He stared at her tears, as if he were fascinated by the sight of them. And sighed. *"Bene."*

She buried her face in her hands. She was aware of every breath of his, of the shift and slide of his muscles as he pulled up his legs. She wanted to burrow into his embrace and sob like one of her students.

But how could he erase the hurt when he was the one who had caused it?

"Pia, was I rough?"

The tenderness in his voice almost broke her. "No." The aftermath of her climax still made her body clench. "Yes, but I wanted it just as much as you did. I'm not breakable."

His rough exhale said he'd been horribly worried about her answer. His worried gaze said he found no solace in it. "Not breakable, *cara mia*. Fragile." He stared at his own hands as if looking for answers as to how to handle her there. He fisted them and she knew it was to stop himself from reaching out to her.

That he knew something was wrong between them offered no relief to the ache in her chest. Why hadn't he fixed it, she wanted to ask. Wasn't that what he was good at?

He ran a hand over his face. "Pia, whatever it is that's bothering you, we will work through it. I... I admit that I have a problem with delegation at work. And I'm willing to find some middle ground."

"It might be a little late now," she said, hating the dejection in her voice.

He stilled. "What do you mean?"

"Why are you tender with me only before or after sex, Raphael? Why do you hide away, closet your emotions, shut me down when we're not engaged in intimacy?"

This time, she definitely didn't imagine the guilty look in his eyes. "You're imagining things. I told you I'm not a man of sweet words."

She snorted. And the bitterness in that sound appalled her. Was that what he had done to her? Had he achieved what Frank hadn't? How could it be love when it hurt so much? "Please don't insult my intelligence. You blow hot when it comes to sex and then cold the rest of the time. You twist me in knots. I'm not allowed to comment on your work life—"

"I just admitted that I have a problem."

"I'm not allowed to talk about what is going on with Allegra. I'm not allowed to mention your father. Damn it, Raphael, I know half the things that are going on in your life because of your mother."

He cursed hard and long. "She has upset you. I should've known. Pia, there's nothing between me and Allegra. Do you have such little faith in me?"

"She did not upset me. *Your* actions did. God, Raphael, when were you going to tell me that you're using our up-coming wedding, using me to deny Allegra even visiting rights to Alyssa? You want me to be a mother to your little girl, but I'm not allowed a say in it?"

"I will not force you to be a mother if you don't—"

"I love your daughter!"

"Then what is the problem?"

"It's your assumption that I will play along with what-ever you have mapped out for us, your inability to include me in anything important in your life. All you want from me is sex. It's the only reason it took me this long to fig-ure it out."

"Figure what out, Pia?"

"That you began retreating from me since I told you I loved you. I guess the guilt was too much for even you."

"What guilt?"

"The guilt of making me fall in love with you, the guilt you feel when I look at you with adoring eyes, the guilt of hiding the fact that you only asked me to marry you because I come with a hefty stock option in Vito Automobiles."

She thought he would explode with anger. But his silence only confirmed his guilt. It skewered the last ray of hope she had nourished that there would be a different explanation, that there could be another reason.

Some fantasy that she hadn't known she had bought into that gorgeous, powerful men like Raphael Mastrantino could fall for plain, geeky, shy nobodies like her.

And now she was pathetically self-pitying too.

"Pia, I was attracted to you from the first night. And you to me." The resignation in his voice delivered the final crack against her heart. He wasn't even denying her allegation.

"According to your mother, you attract more than half the female population in Milan, if not Italy. But I don't think you'd consider marrying them all."

"No. I admit that when Gio proposed it—"

"Of course Nonno talked you into it." She banged her head into the door behind her. The urge to do violence instantly died when her head pounded.

"*Dio mio, Pia!* Stop acting like a child!"

"When have you or Gio treated me like an adult? I obviously don't inspire him to high levels of confidence in myself. Clearly, he knew that it was a facade. Was it the stock that worked finally? Or was it the fact that with the stock in hand, as the uncontested CEO of VA, you've reached heights that your father never could. You could prove to yourself and the world that you're not him. That you could never be weak like him. Have you sold yourself to Gio just to prove that you're incapable of loving, Raphael?"

Raphael pushed up to his feet with an athletic grace she loved and hated and pulled her up with him. When she'd have pushed away from the door, he caged her there with his body. The scent of their intimacy was still thick in the air, a potent mixture that made longing rush through her. "The only thing Gio sought to do was to protect you…"

"From the likes of Frank, *si*? Because I'm naive and plain and will fall for any sweet-talking rogue, like I fell for you, *si*? I get it. He could have just tied up the stock in your name, couldn't he? He could have told me not to fall for anyone because it is only the Vito fortune that is valuable about me."

"Pia, that's not true."

"That's what your actions have made me believe, Raphael," she said softly. "That's what hurt the most. He didn't have to barter me to you as if I were cattle he couldn't wait to get rid of."

Raphael cursed. "He did that because he thought I needed you too."

"Then he is a foolish old man. Because you don't need anybody, least of all a naive idiot like me. Congratulations, Raphael, you have the company, you have the world's adoration, and you have proof that you'll never give something as weak as love any place in your life, like the rest of us. But you've lost me."

Tears catching her throat, Pia pushed away from him.

"Do not walk away from this. Talk to me. Tell me what you need from me. This is the night of our engagement party. There are two hundred people arriving even now."

"All these weeks I was desperate to hear those words from you. I was… I really needed you, Raphael. You will protect me from the big bad wolves of the world. You will triple and double my stock value in VA. You will ply me with expensive, breathtaking gifts. You will seduce me long into dawn. You will pleasure me until I don't know my own name. But you can't love me, can you? You were right all along. It's just not in you." Poison spewed from her lips and Pia couldn't seem to stop herself. And for this, for turning her into this, she truly hated him. "I thought it was only words you weren't capable of."

"I understand that you're upset. But you're being far too cynical about it."

"Shouldn't you be happy that I see the world now as you see it?"

"Nothing has changed."

"No, everything has changed, Raphael. Don't you see? *I* have changed. My perception of *you* has changed. In my eyes, you're no better than Frank."

He reared back as if she had hit him. His nostrils flared, his jaw became tight. "You do not mean that."

"He cooked a friendship with me, pretended to love me because I was an easy mark he could siphon cash out of. You proposed marriage, you bought me with a ring for the same reason. Ergo, you are just like Frank."

A paleness seemed to pool beneath his olive skin. His hands folded, he shrugged. "If you can think that of me, you're right. There's nothing left between us to fix."

Tears clawed up her throat, but she was damned if she would cry again in front of him. Her chest hurt, her limbs trembled. And suddenly Pia knew why it hurt so much, why it felt as if a part of her was being wrenched away.

Why even the worst words from Frank hadn't given her a millionth of this pain. Why it was utterly important that she preserve her pride in front of Raphael while she had flailed like an idiot in front of Frank.

Because his betrayal felt like he'd taken her heart and pounded it into pieces. Because it felt like she would never stop loving him and yet she could never bear to live with him.

She wrapped her arms around herself. "Please tell your cohort that the engagement is off. I can't bear to be near you right now. Tell Gio that I will see him again when he stops hanging that stock sign around my neck for every eligible man to look over. Maybe Gilda didn't sacrifice herself for love, Raphael. Maybe she just wanted freedom from the Duke and her father. And that was the only way she could have it."

CHAPTER FIFTEEN

YOU'RE NO BETTER than Frank.

Weeks after she had spoken them, Pia's words burned holes through Raphael's head.

For the first week or so, he had held on to the anger.

How could she even think that he was the same as that bastard who had deceived her, who had used her for his greed? If he was so low in her estimation, there was no point in them continuing the relationship.

By the third week, his anger had drained away and all that remained was a gnawing sensation in his gut. A burn in his throat. *Dio*, her accusations were a nail continually scraping at his flesh.

But even beneath the hurt, he knew the dread that she was right. At least from where she stood.

He could hardly sleep for the regrets that ate through him all hours.

Even after Frank had hurt her, Pia had never wished him harm. But she'd been so angry, so cynical that day.

So hurt by his actions…

His first thought of even having a relationship with her had begun with Gio's proposal in mind. That he had felt guilty about it, just as she had perceptively realized, was also true.

As days had flown by in the buildup to their engagement party, and the more they were entrenched in each other's lives, the more he had realized that she deserved so much that he could not give.

It was why he had withdrawn from her. Why he had struggled for the first time in his life with the idea that he was inadequate for the role he wanted to play. Nothing and no one had ever prepared him to receive such unconditional acceptance, such unadulterated affection.

And instead of telling her the truth, instead of admitting to his mistakes when she had confronted him, he had pushed her away.

I needed you, Raphael, so much.

The most important person in his life, and he hadn't been there for whatever it was she had needed from him.

He wanted to cherish Pia; he wanted to give her everything she wanted. *Dio mio*, he wanted to be able to love her.

No, not just be able to…

He did love her. He'd been so caught up in his own insecurity that he hadn't realized that he wanted her happiness above everything else in the world, even above his own.

Instead of telling her that, instead of sharing his crisis of faith in himself, he had alienated the best thing that had ever happened to him. Crushed the heart of the one woman, the only person who had seen the real him, who had loved the true him.

I want you, Raphael. Just you.

This time, her words filled him with elation, with energy. This time, instead of pulling away the ground from underneath him, he realized how fortunate he was to have found Pia.

How incredible it was that such a generous woman had seen something in him that was worth loving. That he had been given a chance to love her in return, to spend the rest of his life knowing that whether he succeeded or failed at another business venture, whether he remained hard and unyielding or not, Pia would always love him.

That was how she was made.

And, *maledizione*, he had hurt her for loving him.

Refusing to waste another moment, Raphael choppered himself to Gio's estate instead of being stuck in traffic.

"She's not here," Giovanni mumbled from the sitting lounge even before Raphael could ask the question.

Gio looked tired. Raphael took a seat next to him, his throat closing up. "I ruined it all, didn't I?" He buried his face in his hands. "I… I should have never interfered. I shouldn't have forced—"

"I never intended to hurt her, Gio. I have been a fool, ten times everything you told me I was becoming. But I didn't listen."

"You see, you and I both misjudged Pia. We thought just because she's soft-spoken and generous to a fault, she needed us to look after her, to treat her as if she were a child. But she is tougher than even my Lucia, I think. Only a strong woman could forgive the hurt we caused her."

Raphael jerked his head up. Hope burned a hole through him. "What do you mean? Is she talking to you again? Has she come back from her…*friend's* house?" He almost choked on that word.

That she had moved to her carpenter friend Antonio's house had been a physical blow.

Even split up as they had been—permanently, in her mind—he knew Pia still loved him. That Pia would never just fall out of love with him.

Still, every time he had thought of her sharing a small studio with him—and it had been every waking minute— a possessive urge to throw her over his shoulder and bring her back to his apartment had overpowered him.

"*Si*, she has returned. She said she was too worried about me but it didn't mean she has forgiven me. I am worried about her."

"Why?"

Gio didn't quite meet his eyes. "I promised her I would stay out of this mess between you and her." He sighed. "So I didn't send for you even though… I cannot say more, Raphael. Are you here to fix your mistakes?"

"*Si*. And to beg her to forgive me, if need be."

"But she's very hurt. If you do not love her, you will do it again."

"Giovanni, trust me this time to get it right. *Per favore*." Yet Gio stared at him doubtfully. When had his reassurance not worked for Gio? What the hell was he not saying?

Had he lost Pia?

He shot up from his seat, his nerves shot to hell for the first time in his life. "Where is she?"

"In her bedroom. I'm sure her nap is done."

And since when the hell had Pia needed to nap in the afternoon? The woman was either studying or carving or walking or making friends or learning Italian.

He was already at the foot of the steps when Gio's words stopped him. "Remember what you did and how much she has to forgive. Do not get angry. Do not let your ego get in the way."

Gio's warning ringing in his ears, Raphael took three stairs at a time, pushed open the door to Pia's bedroom and strode in.

She was standing leaning against the wall, looking out into the balcony and turned immediately when he closed the door behind him with a soft thud.

And paled when her sleep-mussed gaze found him.

Something was different about her, he would have known even without Gio's cryptic warnings.

She seemed to have shrunk three sizes in just a few weeks. Not that she had much weight to lose to begin with. Her hair was piled in that knot tightly over the top of her head and it pulled her skin tighter over her features.

Dio mio, she looked as if a hard breeze could blow her over.

Had he done this to her?

"*Christo*, Pia, what the hell have you done to yourself?"

He rushed to her, desperate for action, desperate to set things to rights.

But she moved back from him, her chin stubbornly tilted. Her mouth narrowed. Only her eyes, her gorgeous brown eyes reflected her emotions. "I would appreciate it if you didn't talk to me as if I were an imbecile. Or better, please leave, if that's all you have to say."

He couldn't bear to have her look at him like that.

Couldn't bear the idea of something being wrong with her. Nausea filled his throat. "Are you ill?" The thought of some unnamed disease doing this to her threatened to take him out at the knees.

"Did Gio ask you here?" Fury flared in her gaze at the thought. "Christ, I told him never again. I told him he wasn't to breathe a word to you and he swore…"

Raphael pulled her roughly into his arms, his heart beating so hard he could hear it in his ears. "*Dio mio*, calm yourself. Gio didn't ask me. I came of my own accord. I came to ask him about you. I came because I couldn't…" He drank her in. "Pia, are you sure you're not ill?"

"Stop saying that. You don't have to make me feel worse than I already do. I know I look a fright…"

"Get over yourself, will you? You are beautiful to me. Always. But it's true that you look like you'll break apart if I press hard."

Some of his panic must have come across because she sighed. A wariness entered her eyes. Still, she stepped back from him. "I'm not ill. Just…" A shrug and she looked away. "What are you doing here? Please Raphael, just for once, respect me enough to leave me alone." Sudden tears filled her eyes. "Seeing you like this…you have no idea how hard it is for me.

I have some things to think through, some decisions to make. Then we can talk, *si*?"

He inclined his head. A lead weight sat on his chest. "But I have something to say to you. Will you hear me out?"

"*Si*. As long as you give your word that you won't touch me."

He swallowed the punch it was to his chest and nodded. *"Bene."*

Taking her hands in his, he pulled her to a sofa, then released them. Then went on his knees in front of her. The tears she had valiantly tried to hold back fell over onto her cheeks. And she sniffled.

"Please, *bella*. Do not cry. That I did this to you…" Even his throat was burning now. "Pia, I adore you from the bottom of my heart."

She shook her head and he said, "Just one chance, Pia. Let me finish. I…yes, it was Gio who…maneuvered me into this. You were right. He dangled everything I wanted in front of me. I resisted as long as I could and it was hell for me. But the night of his heart attack, I just couldn't deny it anymore. You were right. I felt the inevitable weight of your responsibility on my shoulders. With Gio looking like he did… I couldn't walk away anymore.

"Everything you said about it is true. But Pia, even if he hadn't, there was a connection between us from the first moment. Not just attraction, *cara mia*. Something that went deeper than that. Even with my jaded view of the world, I knew how incredible you were, how giving. Giovanni was right when he said I needed you in my life, just not the other way around. Only I didn't want to acknowledge the connection. I didn't want to see anything deeper at that time. How could I? I have never known a connection like that before.

"Given enough time, I would like to believe that I'd have come around to the same idea. I have to believe that I would have recognized how precious you are. Seen how much happiness, how much peace you brought into my life. Your love humbles me, *cara mia*, reminds me of what is important in life. Strips everything from me and leaves the core of me stronger. And I would spend the entirety of our lives, an eternity, making you happy, if you would give me another chance."

Breaking his word, he kissed her knuckles. He buried his face in her chest. Her heart thudded near his mouth, the scent of her settling deep in his pores. With Pia, he was home. "I love everything about you, *cara mia*. Every inch of you. Every smile of yours."

"I want to believe you, Raphael. I missed you so much too."

It was as if a weight lifted from his chest. He pressed kisses from her wrists to her shoulders and then across her neck, joy filling him to the brim. "Then marry me, Pia. Marry me because I can't go another day without seeing you, without holding you, without kissing you. Marry me because I want to be yours. Pia's Raphael—when I'm with you, I'm the best of myself."

When her tears gave way to sobs and she fell into his arms, Raphael held her tight and uttered useless phrases for he could not bear her pain.

"You made me doubt myself. You made me hate myself. Love should not do that," she whispered, between hiccups.

He clasped her cheeks and stared into her eyes. "*No, cara mia*. It should not. There's nothing in the world that could put a price tag on you. I fell in love with you long before I realized it. I would not change a thing about you, Pia. You have to believe me."

She nodded and wiped her cheeks, sudden resolution in her movements. "Then I have to tell you something too.

And you have to promise that you will tell me what you feel. That whether you get angry or furious or hurt, you will communicate with me. That you won't just shut me down."

Heart beating rapidly, he nodded. "Pia, you can tell me anything."

She drew in a long breath. "I'm pregnant."

He felt dizzy, as if someone had robbed all the air around them. Questions pounded through him, like flies buzzing, and beneath that, a crushing sense of void in his gut.

This was what Gio had been talking about. *Christo*, how long had she known? How long had she been hiding the truth? How long would she have kept it a secret?

"It is yours," she said so softly that his head jerked up.

He gritted his teeth, trying to corral the hurtful things that wanted to get out. "For all my sins, Pia, I never doubted your loyalty, your love."

The betrayed look in his eyes made Pia wish she could change the circumstances. She had never wanted to be the one who deceived him, never wanted to see that disillusionment in his eyes, but if she had told him, with what she'd learned since about Alyssa... All she had held on to was hope.

He was processing it, she knew, running through the emotions. Breath braced, she waited, hoped he wouldn't just cut her off again. Even a furious explosion was preferable to him shutting her down.

"How far along are you?"

"Almost ten weeks. I think it happened that first time."

"I wore a condom."

"They are not foolproof. Raphael, I know it's a shock but—"

He stood up, a sudden energy to his movements. "What was the decision you had to make? Things you had to think through?" Whiteness emerged under his skin. "*Dio mio*, were you just going to leave Italy without telling me, like Lucia did to Gio? Was that my punishment for hurting you, Pia? Is that all your love means?"

Pia wrapped her hands over his shoulders, willing him to look at her. "Raphael, please listen to me. I… I wasn't going to go anywhere. I would have never left Italy without telling you, even if I wasn't pregnant."

His fingers manacled her wrists, emotion tight in his features. "Then why the hell didn't you tell me?"

"Because if I had told you, you would have insisted on us marrying."

"Of course I would have. Do you want our child to be illegitimate?"

"I don't care for that label, seeing as my father carried it his whole life. I love you with everything in me, Raphael. I will love you the rest of my life. But to be married to you knowing that we were together for our child, knowing that you were doing it to protect me and the baby, to be another responsibility to you, it would've killed any love I felt for you…" She shuddered. "I couldn't live like that."

"What if I had never come back, Pia?"

"After my initial anger faded, I couldn't help but hope. Gio told me about how Alyssa wasn't even yours."

When he cursed, she bade him to look at her. "I was the one who held her first. The one she bonded with, the one who she asks for when she has a hurt. She's just as much mine as she's Allegra's. It doesn't matter that biologically I'm not her father."

"The only reason Gio told me, I think, is to give me hope. And he was right. After everything she did to you, that you could love that little girl so much made me hope, Raphael. It told me that I hadn't made a mistake again. It told me that you could love me. And when Gio told me that you had reconsidered Allegra's requests, that you had agreed to supervised visits, it made me fall in love with you a little more."

"I did it after our fight, when I realized how much I had hurt you. Allegra and I hurt each other throughout our marriage. If there was any chance for you to forgive me, to love me again, I realized I needed to be a better man. For you, Pia. You bring out the best in me, *cara mia*."

Pia felt as if she could fly, as if the happiness rushing through her would consume her.

Sinking her fingers into his hair, she pulled his head down and kissed him. His taste sent a familiar pang through her, released an incredible joy.

He loved her. He loved her. She wanted to shout the words to the world.

He pushed away from her, his breathing rough, his gaze still hurt. "Is this what you needed to talk to me about?"

She nodded, glad that he was talking, working through his emotions with her. "The first test was negative. Then I had some—" heat piled over her cheeks "—bleeding for a day. I thought it was my period finally. But apparently some women bleed even when pregnant. Finally I went to see a doctor and she confirmed it."

He hugged her tight, so hard that for a few seconds Pia couldn't even breathe. "And now? Has it stopped? Is it a danger to you or the baby?"

"No. I still can't keep anything down, which is why I lost so much weight and I have to call her if anything happens."

Raphael sighed. He should have been there with her. "When did you see the doctor?"

"The day after we…the day after everything fell apart."

Lifting her into his arms, he sat down on a chaise and pulled her into his lap. His hands crawled to her midriff, and sure enough, he could feel the barely there curve of her stomach. A wash of contentment settled over him. "It has been rough on you?"

She nodded and burrowed into his chest. "I have been suffering through this horrible nausea. For a while there, I couldn't eat even a cracker for fear of…" She cringed and he smiled.

"Will you forgive me? For not being there when you needed me."

Smiling, she kissed his jaw and then his mouth. "Raphael, I love you from the bottom of my heart. There's no need for forgiveness if you truly believe that you want to spend the rest of your life with me."

"You still doubt me?"

The minx shrugged.

He pushed to his feet and carried her to the bed. He crawled over her, joy beating in his chest. "Then I will have to spend the next few months convincing you that I do. That without you, my life is barren, hard, cold."

"Are you sure you aren't talking about your bed?"

"That too," he whispered before taking her mouth in a hard kiss.

His world for the first time in his life was complete. His family was complete. And he felt utterly loved for just the man he was.

* * * * *

MILLS & BOON

Coming soon

BOUND TO THE SICILIAN'S BED
Sharon Kendrick

Rocco was going to kiss her and after everything she'd just said, Nicole knew she needed to stop him. But suddenly she found herself governed by a much deeper need than preserving her sanity, or her pride. A need and a hunger which swept over her with the speed of a bush fire. As Rocco's shadowed face lowered towards her she found past and present fusing, so that for a disconcerting moment she forgot everything except the urgent hunger in her body. Because hadn't her Sicilian husband always been able to do this—to captivate her with the lightest touch and to tantalise her with that smouldering look of promise? And hadn't there been many nights since they'd separated when she'd woken up, still half fuddled with sleep, and found herself yearning for the taste of his lips on hers just one more time? And now she had it.

One more time.

She opened her mouth—though afterwards she would try to convince herself she'd been intending to resist him—but Rocco used the opportunity to fasten his mouth over hers in the most perfects of fits. And Nicole felt instantly helpless—caught up in the powerful snare of a sexual mastery which wiped out everything else. She gave a gasp of pleasure because it had been so long since she had done this.

Since they'd been apart Nicole had felt like a living statue—as if she were made from marble—as if the flesh and blood part of her were some kind of half-forgotten dream. Slowly but surely she had withdrawn from the sensual side of her nature, until she'd convinced herself she was dead and unfeeling inside. But here came Rocco to wake her dormant sexuality with nothing more than a single kiss. It was like some stupid fairy story. It was scary and powerful. She didn't *want* to want him, and yet . . .

She wanted him.

Her lips opened wider as his tongue slid inside her mouth—eagerly granting him that intimacy as if preparing the way for another. She began to shiver as his hands started to explore her—rediscovering her body with an impatient hunger, as if it were the first time he'd ever touched her.

'Nicole,' he said unevenly and she'd never heard him say her name like that before.

Her arms were locked behind his neck as again he circled his hips in unmistakable invitation and, somewhere in the back of her mind, Nicole could hear the small voice of reason imploring her to take control of the situation. It was urging her to pull back from him and call a halt to what they were doing. But once again she ignored it. Against the powerful tide of passion, that little voice was drowned out and she allowed pleasure to shimmer over her skin.

Continue reading
BOUND TO THE SICILIAN'S BED
Sharon Kendrick

Available next month
www.millsandboon.co.uk

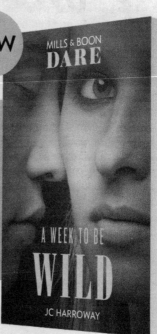

LET'S TALK
Romance

For exclusive extracts, competitions
and special offers, find us online:

f facebook.com/millsandboon

⊙ @millsandboonuk

🐦 @millsandboon

Or get in touch on 0844 844 1351*

For all the latest titles coming soon, visit
millsandboon.co.uk/nextmonth

Want even more
ROMANCE?

Join our bookclub today!

'Mills & Boon books, the perfect way to escape for an hour or so.'

Miss W. Dyer

'Excellent service, promptly delivered and very good subscription choices.'

Miss A. Pearson

'You get fantastic special offer and the chance to get books before they hit the shops'

Mrs V Hall